Gareth Cadwallader

States of Man

New Stories

WriteSideLeft
September 2019

WRITESIDELEFT

ISBN: Print: 978-1-9161011-0-4

ISBN: eBook: 978-1-9161011-1-1

ISBN: Audiobook: 978-1-9161011-2-8

Compilation & Cover Design by S A Harrison
Photo by Steve Hunt

Published by WriteSideLeft UK

www.writesideleft.com

Contents

Also by **Gareth Cadwallader**

Watkins & Co–a novel

Prologue: The Rise and Fall of John Holms

Peggy stood on the balcony of the hotel room in Avignon and, with a stamp of her foot, threw her wedding ring into the street below. Laurence had been raving up and down the Riviera for two weeks solid and she couldn't—wouldn't—take any more. She felt sure he'd had a premonition about John Holms and that was why he'd reacted that way. But then it was the only way he knew how to react to anything. In a café overlooking the rocky coastline he had smashed up all the tables and chairs, throwing bottles and glasses through the windowpanes. In St Tropez, he'd stood her on a table-top and torn her clothes off in front of all the diners. He'd started hitting her, bruising her face; he'd never done that before. Days and sleepless nights of continuous drinking only made him angrier—about everything. He took her clothes and set them on fire on the beach below their house in Pramousquier where they'd gone bathing naked with John and Dorothy when

5

they'd first met them. He held her on the floor until she sobbed so hard she could no longer resist and then stood on her and stamped his feet all over her. All this she'd put up with before in one way or another. He was just a child. But then he pushed her down the concrete steps of the house.

'My God! You could have killed me!' she screamed.

He turned away and slammed the door behind him. And she ran through the woods to the cabin where they were staying to find John and Dorothy and demand that they take her away. She sent them ahead to Avignon, booked and paid for the train and a hotel room for them.

Laurence was glad to see them go; he saw it as his victory. He'd had a terrible fight with John, trying to knock his brains out with a pewter candlestick. John was a big man, and an athlete, who'd won the Military Cross and was quite capable of subduing Laurence, but Dorothy had been traumatised. She was convinced Laurence was going to kill them all. As soon as Peggy saw Laurence was at work in his studio, she bribed the gardener to drive her to the station and caught the train to Avignon. Of course, when Laurence discovered she was gone he was perfectly capable of extracting the details from the gardener and came after them.

Dorothy saw him coming down the main street like a gunfighter. She was in a panic. She insisted the three of them shimmy down a drainpipe and escape down the alley behind the hotel.

Peggy loved to dance with John. That's how it had started. He was so tall she could nuzzle her head against his chest, just below his heart. He could move each muscle independently; he could hold her head perfectly still against him while dancing with his hips and shoulders. On the first night, she'd ended up dancing on the table, just as when Sylvia Plath would be 'stamping and he was stamping' when she first met Ted, and screamed to herself, thinking, 'oh! to give myself crashing, fighting' to him. That was what had set Laurence off. He didn't even know that John had pressed her against the stone walls of the restaurant and kissed her.

John had been living with Dorothy for almost a decade. He'd spent a year in agony drawing her away from her previous lover, carrying a handgun to use either on himself or the other man—he was never sure which. The emotional drama exhausted him— permanently. From the moment he'd won her, decisions were beyond him. He'd never got around to marrying her; never got around to telling her he'd fallen out of love. She was his best friend, but he'd lost all interest in her, sexually speaking. She lived in a perpetually frantic state of trying to reignite his interest. Even so, when Peggy arrived in Avignon, Dorothy had no idea that she was already John's lover.

Some friends of Dorothy's wrote to say they were travelling over from England and would she join them during their stay in Paris.

'Oh, you must go,' John said.

The lawyers were still fighting over the terms of the divorce and custody over the two children, and Peggy was restless and depressed. As soon as Dorothy left, Peggy and John decided to get away. They toured around the Var and Midi. They took a train through a blizzard to Vienna where the city was frozen and there was no coal. They stayed in bed the whole time.

John was the first person Peggy had ever met who considered it perfectly normal to spend all day reading and all night drinking and talking about what he'd read. She was a woman of leisure because she had inherited a vast trust fund of imperial dollars, whereas he was idle through inability to decide what to do. Though he did nothing, his taste and judgment were universally regarded as perfect. He entranced her by reciting hours of poetry he knew by heart. He could talk all night about his ideas for writing fiction or criticism, but he'd invariably exhausted his interest by the time he sat at his desk with a pen in his hand. He was like a giant king of a fairy people who lived on vaporous ambrosia breathed out of the air—and copious quantities of alcohol.

Once, when Peggy and John were staying in Paris, Dorothy surprised them in bed together. She stood at the end of the bed and screamed and beat Peggy on the soles of her feet with a toilet brush until they both collapsed weeping. John, who had fled the room, returned to make peace. Dorothy had decided to return to England, where she was believed by one and all to be the long-standing Mrs Holms. She couldn't go back unmarried; she would be a pariah. She hounded John, insisting that he marry her.

Peggy's divorce from Laurence hadn't come through yet—a few months later, she'd have married John at the drop of a hat and put an end to this nonsense.

After weeks of vacillation, John suddenly caught a train back to Paris and married *Dorothy* before he could change his mind for the hundredth time. His father, who disapproved of his son's idleness, gave him a very modest annual allowance of a few hundred pounds that he and Dorothy had been getting by on for years. Now he arranged to transfer it all to his new wife…and live off Peggy's vastly greater income.

Dorothy also wanted John to edit her biography of the man, obscure then and now long-forgotten, away from whom John had seduced her. She'd been waiting for his comments since before they'd met Peggy. It was driving her mad. John was depressed about not having even started the task when, in truth, he had nothing else to do. To galvanise himself, he promised an article to a journal in London, and proposed to Peggy that they take a long trip with Dorothy's manuscript and his own plan to finally write something.

Peggy's mother had always bought her a new car every year. They'd been driving around the Continent in a gorgeous Delage, but now they bought themselves a Citroen and headed north on a thousand-mile circuit through Germany and Scandinavia. In the back seat they had Peggy's daughter and maid, and her mongrel bitch, Lola, stretched across the sill of the rear window. Perhaps they thought Norway and Sweden would be as dense with Citroen garages and stocks of spare parts as they were with forests. They drove up the coast shuttling from ferry to ferry, driving up wobbly planks of wood to board the little boats, and on unmade tracks across farm fields, stopping to open and shut gates. They drove for hours without seeing another vehicle, much less a Citroen dealership. They travelled, as they lived, heedless of consequences. But the only accident that occurred was Lola getting pregnant in Trondheim.

Sitting in bed for two days next to Peggy in her red negligee, John finally read through Dorothy's manuscript. To Peggy it felt like a triumph, to have coaxed him into action, and even more so to finally shake off the lingering presence of Dorothy in their relationship.

It didn't turn out that way. When Dorothy opened the package containing her manuscript, the first thing that fell out was a red feather from Peggy's knickers. This only served to open a new and more resentful phase in Dorothy's campaign to make John as miserable as she was.

On their way back to the South, John hit on the idea of staying for a while in Bavaria. He felt he could get to grips with the article he'd promised to write. In Munich, they bought a phonograph and lay in bed listening to music or went out to the opera. He never wrote the article.

They lived in a permanent state of boredom and restlessness. Peggy put John's inanition down to the fact that he never met his intellectual equal. For several years they seemed to follow Picasso around, without ever meeting, triangulating between Paris, the South of France and eastern Spain. Peggy shared his fascination with the bullfight, and they lived as 'strangers to premeditation', just as his friend Jaime Sabartes described Picasso, 'his whole entity being restless.' Once John drove Peggy into Spain for a day trip and they enjoyed themselves so much they stayed for ten days—with no luggage.

John's character combined perfect aesthetic judgment with chronic indecisiveness. They spent months looking for a perfect house to rent in Paris. They signed a lease on a house which John found too noisy. They lined the walls with cork, then immediately abandoned it to the man Peggy would eventually take back to America as her lover and moved into the tall thin house overlooking a reservoir that Georges Braque had had built for himself.

That summer, they toured Brittany failing to find the right place to rent, then went to join Giorgio Joyce in St Jean de Luz on the Spanish Basque coast. There, John read and talked and drank all day and climbed the cliffs and dove from prodigious heights into the sea, having consumed the same quantity of alcohol as Peggy's body weight, it often seemed.

He drove their new Delage as though he were flying her across Provence and Lombardy; to Florence, Assisi and Venice. In a blizzard in the Apennines, he only just managed to push the car, teetering at the edge of a sheer drop, back onto the road using his scarf to gain some traction under one of the front wheels. They lived in this state of reckless innocence, somehow never thinking that it must end in an inevitable encounter with a snake, in a tree, in the reeds beside an Arcadian stream, or, in John's case, in a rabbit hole.

One summer, after years of criss-crossing the Continent, they found themselves driving around the West Country of England. Perhaps John had forgotten where he was trying to get away from. As usual, they were failing to find the perfect place to rent. He had never felt able to take Dorothy home, and now, when he visited his parents to negotiate Dorothy's annual allowance, Peggy had to stay in a nearby hotel.

When they got back to Paris, they realised they had seen the perfect place after all and arranged to lease Hayford Hall. It lay at the western edge of Dartmoor, formal gardens running into the wild, rocky moorland. They lived there for two summers, with a procession of houseguests.

Until she met Douglas, neither ever seriously considered being unfaithful to the other, but they suffered terrible, recurring episodes of jealousy. Perhaps Dorothy had set the tone, turning up at their home, screaming at their guests that they had no right to befriend such a terrible woman.

One evening in a café in Paris, Peggy saw Laurence come in and went across to sit for a while with his party. John went berserk and Emily Coleman had to walk him around the streets for most of the night to gradually calm him down. Emily, who had introduced Peggy to John, had been in love with him from the moment she first saw him and would be till he died.

Emily was always with them, unless she had just left or was just about to arrive. Emily could sit up all night listening to John, long after Peggy had had to give up and go to bed. Often, though she was too exhausted to stay awake, Peggy would be too anxious to sleep and would lie wide-eyed and twitching until he came to bed at four or five in the morning. Once she got up in the early hours to find John and Emily reading Kafka in the bath.

They loved to ride on the moor. There were herds of wild and semi-tamed ponies, but only a couple of decent horses for riding. John rode the best one. When Emily was there, she was always nagging him to let her take it; it drove Peggy mad. The saddles slipped, the bridles were frayed, none of the stirrups were ever even, but they galloped across the rocky, boggy moorland as fast as they could for as long as they could. They were given their warning when John rode into a bog and barely got out, dragging the horse out behind him. A couple of weeks later his horse stumbled in a rabbit hole while at a full gallop, throwing John and dislocating his wrist.

This marked the first fall of John Holms.

Somewhere along their journey, Peggy had realised that she was protected by her wealth, as vast and impenetrable as Satan's shield. But for John, a rarefied Dionysian being, whose hubris had been heedless and unrelenting, it was not enough to fall only once. There was a second snake in the garden.

Douglas was that second snake.

He had captivated Peggy the moment she first saw him. Taller even than John, a man of the world, he dressed in a gentlemanly style and admired her clothes and noticed the efforts she made to overcome her 'dog nose'. The only time she'd been unfaithful to Laurence was with John. Now, almost immediately upon meeting Doug, she decided she would make him her lover. In their six years together, John had managed to write one poem. Doug, a barely viable commercial publisher of *avant-garde* fiction had had a whole book of his poetry published. He read his poems to them, asking for comments. John found one line in one of the poems that he quite liked.

Compared to John, Doug was a man of action; exactly as close to and as far from John's intellectual and aesthetic saintliness as she wished to stray.

She wrote to Doug proposing a liaison in London, but he was away travelling. She goaded John with

Doug's accomplishments and good looks. He turned into a growling, spitting monster, stripping her naked and making her stand in their open window while he threw glassfuls of whisky in her eyes while he decided whether to push her out. She had gone too far. She knew she would have to wait. Something told her it wouldn't be for long.

John Holms's wrist was set, broken and reset, but never completely healed. He was persuaded to have an operation under general anaesthetic to remove a calcified growth. Peggy returned from a trip to Paris to be told he was going in for the surgery the following morning. He sat up with friends drinking through the night. He'd already postponed the operation once on account of flu; he didn't want to mess the doctors around again. Perhaps he, too, sensed that the lethal venom was already in his blood. The doctors came to their London home to do the operation. Once they'd administered the anaesthetic they insisted Peggy leave the room.

The whole procedure should have taken half an hour. She sat outside, wide eyed and twitching the way she'd waited for him in bed. Her mind flashed back and forth between images of John recovered and a future life with Doug. She sat there for over an hour and during that time the pictures of Doug became clearer and more solid. She imagined being consoled by him, driven to his home in Sussex, living with a man of the world, a man who was her intellectual inferior, whose life she could shape, now she had been shaped by John. Originally, she had imagined a short affair, nothing more. If John had promised to cast off Dorothy and asked her to marry him from his bed just before the anaesthetic had been administered, she would have said 'Yes, yes, yes.' But an hour later when it was inexplicable that the doctors hadn't reappeared to congratulate themselves, it seemed obvious to her that his work on her was done.

In any case, he never woke up.

The Fall 1984

I was an outstanding footballer as a boy. I could sprint from a standing start. In an instant, could shift my weight one way and take the ball the other. Somehow everything happened at the speed I dictated. Gaps appeared, passing lanes opened, defenders stepped out of position all just at the moment I was ready to take advantage. Without realising it I could see the whole pitch; knew where everyone was and where they were going next. I was not a big boy—I was often playing with and against boys a foot taller than me— but I was elusive. And tough. I could be knocked down but I would always get up. I might have a split lip, but I would cut through the defence and score. I watched the older boys, the boys who already had contracts with clubs. I could see what they were doing. It was as though there was a commentary running alongside their actions that only a few of us could understand. When I saw a move I'd never seen before, I could draw what I'd seen into my muscles and joints and, the next afternoon, after school, it would be waiting there, coiled and ready to spring out into the world. Once, when I was playing in a practice match one of the first-team players joined in. He had a swagger even when no-one was watching—maybe there was never a moment when no-one was watching him. He left me on my backside as he slid the ball across me and then through my legs, touching the ball four times in the blink of an eye. He came straight back to pick me up and apologise. 'I know how to do that now,' I said, and he smiled in a way that let me know that I was one of 'them.'

My father liked having a son who was good at sports, who was talked about as a future professional footballer. But he was dead set against it. 'He's a bright boy,' he'd tell anyone who asked him. 'Football's no career for him.' There was a kind of Cold War between us. I knew that I was going to play football. I knew how many goals I would score for Chelsea and how many trophies I would win. I would win thirty caps for England and play in the World Cup. My father would only shake his head whenever we saw a player injured or unavailable through injury or dropped through nothing more than the Manager's whim. 'That's the end of his match.' 'That's the end of his season.' And when my best friend Sy did his anterior cruciate ligaments, 'That's the end of his career, then. He'll be grateful for bar work, I suppose.' I was so angry with him about that, I could hardly speak to him for a fortnight.

One of the things we liked to do together was stay up late and watch the Old Grey Whistle Test. It was a combined rebellion against my mother, who stood for routine, homework and early bedtimes; harmless enough, but it felt reckless. I was never closer to my father. I was too young to go out to rock concerts, so this was the closest I got to seeing Siouxsie Sioux or Spandau Ballet in the flesh. I can remember on nights when we'd watch together, snuggling against his shoulder, something neither of us would have contemplated at any other time.

One night, on the Old Grey Whistle Test, they had a set by a Manchester band. My father thought it was dreadful. He was snarling sarcastically at the screen. On the John Peel show on the radio, I might have dismissed the music as noise. But there was something electrically exciting about the performance.

Even watching a programme I enjoyed, I found it hard to sit still for more than a few minutes. There was always a ball of some kind in a corner of the living room; a tennis ball or a squidgy mini-football, even a balloon would do. I would juggle the ball as I wandered round the sofa and coffee table, watching the television. I had a sort of radar system that tracked a moving ball at the periphery of my field of vision. I didn't need to look. I always knew where it was, just from the feel of it on my foot. I could shuffle my feet three or four times between touches, softly adjusting my balance so that my contact with it was always under control. The boys called me The Snake; I could slide between dangers and strike swiftly whenever an opponent was on his heels or showed a little too much of the ball.

I was juggling behind the sofa when the presenter, Andy Kershaw, introduced The Fall. I'd never heard of them. The music started with a harsh blare. There was no sign of a band. The stage was full of people in fancy dress, pretending to swallow a length of ribbon. Then they started dancing to droning guitar music. A voice, obviously Mancunian, from out of the camera shot was chanting something about the Lay of the Land. A man, it was definitely a man, in a brown outfit with one breast showing, and brown streaks on his face, started dancing. Though I don't think I'd ever seen ballet before, it was obvious that he was a kind of ballet dancer. He was joined first by two women, or at least one was definitely a woman: although she was dressed in the same mud colour as the first man, and had an androgynous Mohican hairdo, I immediately noticed she had full breasts. They moved on the balls of their feet, there was a poised, gliding motion to their steps, and they held elaborate, extended balances.

My father started moaning about 'queers' and 'noise' and 'artsy rubbish'. I realised I'd let the ball drop to the carpet. I was standing still, wide eyed. Suddenly, I was seized with the impulse to rise up on my toes and emulate the dancers. I balanced on the ball of one foot, stretching my other leg out behind me. I could turn in this position in a slow spin. To my delight, my father started laughing. Of course, this egged me on. I did a little scissor kick and landed with my knees bent and my arms out wide. We both started giggling hysterically. Out of the corner of my eye I saw another dancer come on, with long hair and ruffles on a blue blouse so that, again, I couldn't tell if it was a man or woman. He or she wore a large green cap and red leggings and moved as though on tip toe. He and the first man hopped about on one set of toes pointing the other foot. I started doing the same. Then they stood on one leg with an arm curled in front of them like a cobra's head and started slowly turning on one foot. I could do this perfectly, even anticipating a little. My father was rolling on the sofa with laughter. As the dancer in the red leggings and I were both turning our backs to each other, I saw at the edge of my spinning vision that the seat was missing from the red leggings. The centre of the screen was filled with what my father later called 'his bloody great bare arse.' I only caught a glimpse of it as I spun away. I had never seen anything like it on television. I'd never seen anything like it, full stop. If you'd have asked me beforehand, I would not have believed it was possible. My head and torso froze in a combination of thrill and incomprehension. But my legs were committed to the twist, and my left foot caught under the coffee table. Under the drone of the guitars I heard the groan of something being torn beyond its capacity to stretch.

My father thought I was still screeching with laughter as I lay rocking on the sofa. I couldn't feel anything specific, there was something huge and misshapen where my ankle and foot should have been, a frightening self-consuming terror spreading up my leg and back, gripping the base of my skull.

Years later I would think of Goya's monster eating the white flesh of his own child whenever the memory of that moment came back to me. I knew how bad it was when I looked up to see my mother's bloodless face and bulging frightened eyes staring down at me. I knew in that instant it was all over. I didn't need to look down. I never saw it at all, only the X-ray. My father thought it was the nakedness on the screen that had upset her.

'His leg,' she screamed. 'His leg. Look at his leg. My poor darling.'

I don't remember anything else until I woke up in hospital the next day in traction. A spiral fracture and serious ligament damage.

'Well, now you'll be able to concentrate on your studies,' my Dad told me, trying to be positive, trying not to sound like a victor.

I hated him for that. I stored that anger for years and years. I remember telling my first wife about it.

'Well, you wouldn't have become a Barrister, if you hadn't had that accident,' she said.

But I snarled at her, 'You're wrong. I could've. I could've done both.'

And I found out later that I hated her, too.

The memory of that moment lies dormant for months but re-surfaces unpredictably, with all the anger bubbling over and scalding everyone and everything around me. I dreamt about it last night, though it was my Dad running around with his bloody great bare arse and I was running after him kicking him and kicking him until he fell down sobbing. And, in the way of dreams, it turned out it was me on the ground. And I woke up sobbing. And I had to tell my new wife, who is young and lovely and adores me, what it was all about. She stroked my head and kissed my neck.

'Well,' she said softly in my ear, 'You should be grateful. You wouldn't have got all this padding that I love so much,' she patted my waist, 'or become a High Court Judge, otherwise, would you?'

And I had to admit, she was probably right.

Probable Assault

I just got back from this course on Time Management.
Simplification, that's my take-away. I'm going to
spend the weekend throwing out every piece of junk
in every cupboard and on every square yard of floor,
the freezer, the fridge, everything. And I'm getting a
grip on my diet. I'm doing the two-day fasting thing.
Half a gallon of water a day. And no drinking during
the week. Yeah, all that stuff. Stripping it down.
Living, instead of administering my life. And those
crazy investments I've been talked into; so many I can
never keep track of them. They're all going; I just need
one sensible account. I already started. And as for
asking that new girl in South-Central Sales out on a
date, that is definitely on hold.

Day Two into my new regime. My first fasting day
starts tomorrow. I'm pretty anxious about it. I keep
feeling anticipatory cramps. Then Scruffs calls me up.
Scruffs is our Talent Guru. She's called Scruffs

because of some underwear incident after a 'Social' in the Early Days when we were over in Oakland. Once I took the joke a little too far and she called me out:

'LaSalle, that's not such a great name either.'

My mother thought it was the name of a Running Back she liked, but it turned out she'd misheard it. Anyway, as I always do, I shrugged and smiled a sophisticated little smile and said that I liked its Hispanic vibe.

'It's French,' she said. 'It means Dining Room.'

I always hate it when I meet people who speak French. They have a way of making you feel inadequate. I came out West to get away from people like that.

Anyway, Scruffs said, 'Did you see Francesca leave yesterday; left the building in tears.'

Yeah, I'd heard. I was seriously unhappy about it. She got a new Junior started yesterday. Left him twiddling his thumbs.

'Did you check whether she was in today?'

I hadn't. You think I go around checking whether people have shown up for work?

'She's supposed to be training up…er… what's'isname.'

'Jamal. And No. She isn't in. She just called me. She's taking a week off.'

Unbelievable. This guy, Jamal, he has to be making calls by next Monday. In fact, it's totally not acceptable.

'She's seeing her Doctor.'

Why? She was fine yesterday. There's nothing wrong with her.

'She had a bust up of some kind. With Geraldine. She says she's stressed out.'

Geraldine is the Numero Uno sales rep, with her Ferrari parked a couple of bays down from my Sentra.

'What if I went over and shouted and screamed at Gerry: "You are ruining my fucking life."? Maybe then I'd have to see my doctor. I could really do with a week off, a coupla days at the spa, get my eyebrows and fucking toenails done.'

'I don't think this is helping. You need to take over Jamal's induction.'

I gestured at my screen. I have, like, three thousand two hundred and seventeen tasks waiting to be actioned here. I haven't got time to teach Jamal how to use the speed dial function.

Well, that's just hit the delete button on my fasting day tomorrow. There's only so much I can deal with. I managed to stop by and see Jamal later in the afternoon.

'Hey, Jamal. Sorry I haven't been able to get over to you earlier. Why not let's grab a beer and we can do a little induction over a drink?'

That went pretty well, actually. I had to help him into his Uber at eleven. Told him to come in a bit later in the morning.

God! I feel like my body's been washed up on the beach while my guts are still out at sea. Eighty-seven new tasks waiting to be actioned and one thousand eight hundred and seventy-four overdue, rolled over from yesterday. One of the new ones was an Office Survey follow-up.

While I was away they did this survey in the office. I mean, I'm not making a fuss about being disenfranchised, being, like, virtually one of the Founders of this Company with a single-digit employee number. What do I care? Anyhow, a couple of the tech guys on my team put in suggestions that we set up Napping Areas. What is this? So, they don't have to take naps at their desks, huh? Bad for their posture, or something. I mean, what are evenings for? what are nights for? what is home for? Lorens arrived at my desk, smirking. I knew what he was going to say.

'Maybe it would be more efficient to replace the work pods with bunk beds,' he said. He speaks like a Californian, except for words like "efficient" which he can only say in a European sort of way. He leant across my newly cleared desktop, moved my two-pint water bottle aside and murmured much more threateningly, 'Don't bring any more people who want to take naps into my fucking company, you hear me?'

Normally I don't see Scruffs from one week to the next but this morning she's back again.

'Francesca has a Doctor's Note. She's been signed off for…wait for it…three weeks.'

It took a few moments to sink in. Three weeks! Is there like a fractured femur that someone forgot to mention, or a ruptured Achilles tendon, or something? Three weeks off, for feeling stressed. Christ, I needn't have to work for a year.

'She says Gerry forced her way into her apartment. They were both completely stoned. She remembers screaming at her to leave. She has no recollection of what happened after that.'

'Why did she want to 'force' her way into her apartment for?'

'Oh, come on LaSalle. Do I have to spell it out?'

'Oh my god, you mean it's like a lesbian thing.'

'You are such a moron.'

'Anyway, what's that got to do with us? We don't monitor people's sleeping arrangements.'

'Frankie's woken up the next morning feeling violated. She's writing in a grievance against Gerry. What's more, she's gone to the cops.'

'What! What's it gotta do with the cops?'

'Yeah. It seems like they told her to go home and get over it. Anyway, she's off for three weeks.'

'I've got this guy, Jamal. I need him to start generating numbers. Talk about screwing me over. Thanks Frankie.'

'Once we get the grievance letter, you're gonna have to investigate it.'

'No way. Why me?'

'Because you are Frankie's manager and you are responsible for her well-being and safety at work.'

'Surely not. Do I have the authority to go into the system and change her reporting line? I'm not cut out for investigating relations between women.'

'That's the first evidence of self-awareness I've ever seen from you, La Salle.'

Strangely enough, left to his own devices Jamal got off to a good start, picking up Frankie's calls and even closing some business during the first week.

Lorens cornered me in the car park the next morning. Scruffs had obviously brought him up to speed.

'I need Gerry focused on her pipeline, you hear. I know you need to talk to her but take it easy. She's the difference between us hitting our goals this quarter.'

I sat down with Scruffs and Gerry after I'd had a chance to go through Frankie's grievance letter. Basically, they'd gone out after work with a bunch of other staff. As they'd got gradually drunker and more heavily stoned, Gerry had harassed her, putting her under pressure to go home with her, then insisting on sharing an Uber back to Frankie's place, before forcing her way in. Gerry's a big girl, it wasn't hard to see her doing that. Frankie claimed she'd been asking Gerry to leave her alone for most of the evening; at one point standing outside her apartment building screaming at her to go away.

'I thought it was just a game,' Gerry said. 'She was like that the other times, but it all seemed to work out.'

'Oh, so this wasn't the…er…the first time…the two of you.'

'No, we've had an on-off thing going on for a while.'

'Jesus.' I think I said that quietly enough that no-one heard. 'And...er...it's not really any of my business, beyond a certain point, but would you say that anything of a violent or, what's the word, involuntary nature took place during the night?'

'I have no memory of what happened. But it felt good in the a.m., you know, we kissed.'

'Yeah, okay...that's fine, well, thank you Gerry. We'll have a think about things and come back to you.'

Next morning, I'm rejigging my diary. I'm going to the gym three times a week, but it's Thursday and I haven't got there yet. And I'm thinking I need to combine both my fasting days this week into one. I'm gonna do a super-fast tomorrow; that'll get me back on schedule. The cute woman in South Central is definitely being taken off the back burner and into the deep freeze.

And then Scruffs comes by, like some witch out of Shakespeare, a prophet of catastrophe. First, she wants to set up a workshop on the fucking Napping Zones. She's gonna get me fired roping me into this.

She says Lorens knows all about it and thinks it's a great idea. A great idea to see which idiots put their heads above the parapet, is what it is. She hands me a letter to Frankie she's drafted, with the Doctor's Note attached to it. I skim the Doctor's Note and freeze, my jaw open and every orifice in my body momentarily gaping. After I've regained control of my various valves and sphincters, I manage to say:

'It says "stress arising from sexual assault" here. "Sexual assault," I mean, what does this guy think he's doing. I mean, the least he could have done was say "alleged," huh? And what about non-penetrative; "alleged, non-penetrative sexual assault" feels like the least he could have done. Am I correct in thinking that anything that happened here was more than likely non-penetrative?'

'You're acting like a moron again.'

I've had enough of Scruffs. I have enough problems without my chief advisor and human resources professional calling me a moron. I went to see Lorens.

'Do you know what it says on her Doctor's Note? "Sexual Assault" is what it says. We can't ignore that. What if she gets prosecuted and all we did was give her a rap on the knuckles. If it was anyone else, we'd suspend them while we investigated.'

'No way. Make her get some counselling. I don't want her taking any time off. After the quarter-end, send her on a course, or something.'

I'm seeing Scruffs for about the tenth time this week— I'm gonna have to change my status on Facebook. We have what I would like to think was a firm but friendly conversation with Geraldine.

'Hey, Gerry, you know poor old Frankie's taken things really hard.'

'Yeah, I know,' she says, 'But I just don't know why. I really like her, y'know, and everything seemed to be going okay.'

'Hmm, yeah, right. Well listen, Gerry, y'know how much we all love you, but you know this can't happen again. You realise that, don't you? Nothing like this. Like, ever.'

'Yeah, I'm being more careful.'

Good, I thought that went well, huh, Scruffs? Scruffs thinks we need to follow up in writing. I'm not writing anything. It needs to be documented, she says, in case we ever have to take further action. I'm not taking any further action. You document it, I said.

Major win in the car park late that evening. I was feeling like shit, 'cause I'd just remembered that it was supposed to be my super-fasting day and I'd already eaten about two thousand calories and was on my way to my favourite Viet take-out place. And then who should wave me over but Lorens.

'Putting in the hours, La Salle. Lovin' what you're doing, man. That Jamal, he's a great hire. He's got all the right moves.'

Little did I know at the time how much that would pay off the next morning when Geraldine failed to turn up for work. I got to Lorens's office so fast I didn't have time to put my shoes on.

'Hey Lorens,' I could see he was looking at my feet. 'Fucking Scruffs. She's a walking sabotage factory. She only wrote Gerry a disciplinary yesterday, and this morning—surpri-eese! Gerry's called in sick with the dreaded stress.'

Lorens, who's Dutch and pretty pasty to begin with, went a kind of goat's cheese colour, worked his jaw silently for a few seconds and got up and started to walk out.

'Time to terminate the Napping Pods project, I guess,' I called after him.

Scruffs was gone about thirty minutes later. Suddenly, my chances of getting through the week without being called a moron are on the up 'n' up.

Thursday evening and I'm looking at my desk and I can't see it for paper, coffee cups, a pizza box, several scrunched-up energy drink cans, a pile of bills and other stuff from my apartment. I find a black garbage bag in the cleaner's room and just tip everything in. I figure, if I haven't had to retrieve anything by Tuesday it can all go. I take Jamal out to my gym and a few drinks afterwards. That's all he seems to need to keep him fired up: the human touch, y'know. I have to hand it to him, he does a sub-six-minute mile, pumps three hundred pounds and washes it down with nachos and whiskey sours. Anyway, I ticked off one of my gym visits for the week.

Friday is my super-fasting day, and then at eleven, just as I'm thinking of heading to the gym, Lorens calls and wants me to come out to lunch at Guido's, his favourite Italian. He pats me on my side and tells me I'm putting on weight, then orders carbonara for two and a bottle of Barolo. He's pretty down, starts showing me charts of what's going to happen if Gerry doesn't come back to work—basically, missed targets and a cash squeeze. Says he plans to ask her to come back. Proceed with caution, I say. You're gonna look weak if you give in to her, I say. And we're going to look terrible if we take her back and Frankie starts a prosecution for assault. Yeah, yeah, yeah, he says. He talks me into ordering the tiramisu, and then immediately gets up. He wants to meet back here at seven. He's going to talk to Gerry. It's half past two. I could go home and sleep for a coupla hours. But I promised myself I'd get my outstanding tasks down below eight hundred by the end of the week, and if I get three more hours at my desk I can achieve at least one of my week's objectives.

Lorens is already sitting at the table when I arrive at seven. He gets up and claps his hands.

'Yeah, yeah, great meeting, I think we got it all sorted out,' he says.

I'm wondering how he's done that.

'Yeah, she wants to come back next week. She wants us to erase the disciplinary letter and we're gonna write her an apology.'

'Uh-huh,' I say, feeling like this is not as great as Lorens is making it out to be. His Adam's apple bobs up and down.

'I had this great idea. I think we should fire Frankie. I mean, she's just become a nuisance, and since that Jamal guy started blasting his targets Frankie's become kinda expendable, don't you think?'

I just let the utter stupidity of this idea hover and then sink in the air around us. Let me tell you, these are the moments when guys like me earn our stock options. Because not many people woulda stopped Lorens in his tracks, or even known how to do it.

'Y'know, Lorens, this might not be the perfect moment to make Frankie really pissed off. I mean putting to one side the possibility that she has actually been assaulted by another of our employees. She definitely feels that way, in fact, she has a Doctor's note saying she has been actually assaulted. That we can't deny we've seen. Maybe it would be inviting a kinda hostile response, if we were to fire the alleged victim, and bring back the culprit with garlands and apologies.'

'Really. I thought it was a great idea. What do you think we should do?'

Now he looked like a puppy who'd been slapped for peeing on the carpet when he didn't know any better. You just gotta let these moments hang in the air, if you want the punch to land.

'I think you should give it a week.'

And to my surprise he caved in without even a fight, because I genuinely think he had no idea what to do and all it needed was for someone he trusts to tell him something that took the monkey off his back. He said nothing, but nodded in his Yoda-like way, and ordered another bottle of red followed by grappa. I had a sleepless night in a bed that tilted like a fairground ride in a room that changed shape and size every time I opened my eyes. It took me till Sunday afternoon to feel normal enough to go to the gym and sweat out the last of the toxins.

I'm feeling ready for anything on Monday morning, with only seven hundred and eighty-nine outstanding tasks and a fasting day that's started well with an apple for breakfast. Anything, that is, except seeing a couple of obvious plain clothes cops in reception. I slack the receptionist and find out they're waiting for Lorens. I call him in his car. Yeah, he already knows.

Yeah, it's about Frankie and Gerry. What's he gonna do? he wants to know.

First thing, I write to Gerry, like, a real letter—on paper—signed with a pen, backdated to Friday, suspending her, pending completion of an ongoing investigation into Frankie's grievance and get one of the contractors who won't be here past the end of the week to run it over to the post box in the mall.

I call Scruffs, 'Hey Scruffs, get outta bed, all's forgiven, Lorens wants you back, there's two grand in your hand for signing back on—yeah, yeah and big hugs from Lorens who's really upset and can't forgive himself and wants to say sorry. Yeah, yeah, I know but I need you here in like twenty-five minutes max. Yeah you do need to put your make up on—no, I didn't mean it like that.'

We're back at Guido's for lunch, this time with Scruffs. Do I have to eat pasta again? Lorens doesn't give a damn what I eat. In his very Dutch way, he's getting very emotional, very loud.

'You guys have saved my life. I love you both. I don't deserve you. You saved me from myself.' He's talking in that Dutch way where they do something funny in their throats. 'To think I was going to fire poor Frankie. Sometimes I think I must be a terrible guy.'

'No, no, no,' we say, 'if anything, it's your sensitivity and soft-heartedness that holds you back.'

He nods and holds up his hands in acknowledgement.

'Hey Scruffs, while I remember, I was going to grant this guy another tranche of stock options. Can you do the admin for me?'

'Hey, thanks, Lorens.'

'Hard earned, La Salle, every one of them. And you know what? I'm gonna make you Employee of the Month.'

'Wow, that's amazing Lorens.' That comes with a thousand dollars. Then a thought comes to me. A good thought. 'Hey, Lorens, you know, you should give that to Jamal. His numbers have rescued the whole Frankie situation. He's your future Geraldine replacement, you know that.'

Scruffs gives me a 'taken-aback look' and Lorens does his Yoda nod, and says, 'Good call, La Salle. I like it. Putting the company first. I'll remember that.'

And this seems like a good time to check out, because I can feel the grappa bottle edging its way off the shelf and onto our table.

'Yeah, well, I gotta get back to my desk, guys. I got, like eight hundred outstanding actions sitting there waiting for me.'

I might just as well have jabbed Lorens with a cattle prod.

'Eight hundred fucking Tasks? Man, what d'ya think I pay you for?' He's looking menacing, leaning across the table.

'Yeah, well Scruffs sent me on a course, and since then, all Hell's broken loose.'

'We're investing in your development, and this is what I get in return, huh? This is my business you're messing with. I'll give you to the end of the week to get that down to double digits, you hear me? Get outta here.'

As I get to the door, I'm pretty sure I hear Scruffs saying something about a 'moron' that makes Lorens laugh out loud.

Ah, well. I got my stock options, anyway.

The Real Thing

It was his brother Robbie who'd got Darren playing
Fantasy Football. Not that Robbie played. It'll get you
closer to the staff, Robbie had explained, give you
something to talk to them about. Robbie didn't have
time to talk to the staff personally. The two brothers
owned a software business with an office just off Old
Street. Well, the main office was there, but Darren had
an office a couple of streets away where he could work
in peace and had a place to park his motorbike. He
was responsible for licensing, contracts and collecting
the cash.

For Darren, who had no interest in football, this
had been a minor nuisance to which he'd paid scant
and irregular attention until, around Christmas, he'd
found himself at the top of the league in which many
of the staff and a few of the drinkers at The Griffin
played. Now that he was top of the league, they
looked at him differently, spoke to him differently.
There was respect, yes, but there was also the

45

unspoken accusation: you're a fraud; you know nothing about football.

Since then he'd felt nothing but pressure. He'd been driven by the need to prove he was a deserving leader, that he was *not* a fraud. And he'd stayed on top until now, with a twenty-point lead and just two games to go. One of Robbie's sales reps, Grimesy, was his closest rival, and Grimesy was yet to use his Triple-Captain. This huge fact had weighed on Darren all week, like an unavoidable obstacle that was always standing in his path. Now, at four o'clock on a Friday afternoon, as he had done every Friday since the turn of the year, he gave up on his aged debtors and late deliveries and turned his full attention to his Fantasy Team, and this week's free transfer. For over an hour he went back and forth over a dozen options, entering the data into a vast spreadsheet he'd created, before returning to his original choice. He clicked the *Confirm Transfer* button and let his head sink into his hands. Now he could only think of catastrophic scenarios; own goals, sendings-off, heavy defeats.

It took him twenty minutes to compose himself enough to walk over to The Griffin. His entrance had to be precisely measured. Whereas some players entered the pub thumping their chests, declaring how their team would clean up over the coming weekend, and others sat anxiously over their pints seeking to avoid the subject altogether, Darren, whose team was called Dazzler's Eleven, always tried to look like it could hardly matter less to him how many points his team had scored or whether he'd been usurped.

Grimesy was already there, looking at him over his pint glass like an obsidian-eyed snake.

'Used your Triple-Captain, yet, Grimesy?' Darren greeted him, intending to laugh lightly but not managing.

Before Grimesy could respond, Darren's phone rang. It was Robbie.

'Where the hell are you?'

'In The Griffin. Fantasy League Leadership comes with responsibilities.'

'Have you sorted out that contract, yet?' Robbie was selling Distribution Rights in Asia to a firm in Singapore.

'I'll get straight onto to it on Monday.'

'The hell you will. Hey, Dazzler, you need to wake up. That deal is worth millions to you and me.'

Actually, Darren wanted to say, *it's worth millions to you, Robbie, but quite a lot less to me.* Robbie had arranged a side deal that involved two years of

Strategic Consultancy that doubled the deal value for himself.

'Sort it. Now.' Robbie hung up without waiting for a response.

'He's a dreamer,' Linda complained, placing a Florentine biscuit on the saucer of her coffee cup, and two on Denise's. See could never resist the temptation to try to fatten Denise up a bit.

'When I first met you, you used to call him your Bobby Dazzler.'

'Yeah, but you ended up with the real Bobbie Dazzler, didn't you?'

'Don't be silly, Linda. Nobody's perfect, and they're both good guys in their own ways.'

They sat across the central island in Linda's newly remodelled kitchen. Linda stared out at Denise's new BMW SUV. She held down a three-day-a-week job, and still they couldn't afford a car like that. Denise looked out at Linda's rose border and Japanese azaleas. If she could just pin Robbie down, they could redo the kitchen and get someone in to sort the garden out. But Robbie never stayed still long enough to decide anything—not at home, not for her. Even when he made love to her if felt as though it was while he was on his way somewhere.

'I think he's sweet, your Darren.'

'Sweet like a wildflower that's being blown off somewhere. Full of big ideas but nothing ever amounts to anything beyond his Fantasy Football and his bloody motorbike.'

'This kitchen doesn't look too bad.'

'Yeah, but it's Robbie who makes the money, isn't it?' She even thought of it as Robbie's kitchen, not that he'd ever been in it.

'And your children are…'

'Darren's not interested in the kids. They bore him. They bore me, too, sometimes, but I don't have the option of taking the bike out to clear my head.'

Denise liked the idea of the bike. And the wildflowers.

'You should get him a dog.'

'A what? You've got to be joking.'

'You want to domesticate him, don't you? Get him a dog.'

'It'll be me walking the dog and picking up its shit.'

'Make him walk it. Make him take it in to get it castrated.'

'Oh yeah, I can just see him doing that. This is your worst ever idea Dee. What are you trying to do to me?'

'A man can't ever feel the same way after he's taken his dog in to get castrated. Not about the dog—or anything else.'

'You're crazy,' said Linda, laughing because she was sure now that Denise had been joking all along.

Denise stared out of Darren's office window, lightly tapping her espresso-martini and old-ivory striped fingernails on the small round meeting table. Darren waved his free hand in the air, miming hurry-up hand-signals. He had one of his most egregious aged debtors on the phone and he was reluctant to let him go without extracting a committed payment date.

His heart was beating fast and high in his chest. Denise had never come to his office before. When he put the phone down, she said,

'I was shopping.' She gave him a look to make sure he'd registered that it was more than a casual detour to come to Old Street from the West End. 'I thought you could take me out for a cocktail. It's Friday, after all.'

It was coming up to four o'clock, time to review his Team and make his final transfer of the season. Grimesy had not played his Triple-Captain the previous week. Darren needed to get his own transfer right, and hope Grimesy's captain failed to score a hat-trick. He'd been thinking about it all day, all week, really.

And now here was Denise sitting in his office looking like something out of a magazine.

'Where's Robbie?'

'In the States somewhere. I thought you'd know.' Darren knew he was in Singapore. 'He is just the voice of God in my ear.'

She smiled. She had a slightly wide mouth, with straight lips, and brilliant, straight teeth. He'd never seen her laugh so spontaneously before, without conscious decision, so that her dark eyes lit up.

'He says we're about to come into a lot of money.'

'I have a fairly sizeable administrative cock-up on our Great Leader's part to sort out first.'

This wasn't quite true. He'd sent the complete set of documents over to Singapore that morning, including the ones that had been corrected to say what they should have said in the first place.

'He says you always sort things out. What are you going to spend it on?'

For a moment he thought she'd said 'Who?' He hadn't thought about it, either way. Maybe he'd get himself a new bike.

'What do you dream about?'

He'd always thought of her as a bit too skinny, too reserved, too smart compared to his Linda. But now that she seemed suddenly attainable, she seemed long-limbed, serene, flawless.

'I'm not a very interesting person.'

'I think it's fascinating when a man's dreams are hidden so deep he needs someone else to find them for him.'

'I might be a disappointment on that score.'

'What do you think about when you're riding your motorbike?'

Without a pause, he could answer that: 'Freedom.'

'I don't want to be unfaithful to Robbie.' She was looking across the street again.

His heart started thumping. His chest and throat were tight. He didn't trust himself to speak.

She turned to face him, and said, 'The twins are playing in a tournament tomorrow. Come and keep me company.'

'Football's not my thing.'

'Mine neither,' she laughed again. He felt himself tilt, as though he might lean over and kiss her without really meaning to. 'I'll text you the postcode.'

They walked out together, but she left him at the corner, opposite The Griffin.

'Don't forget to bring a helmet for me.' She lifted her shopping bag. 'I bought a leather suit.' She raised her eyebrows half an inch and turned away. A car was waiting for her.

Half in a daze he wandered into The Griffin, bought a round for the early-starters and made small-talk for a couple of hours while he dealt with his inner turmoil. He wished he was hidden away down in the middle of the league. He wished that Denise had left him alone. But he was top of the league, and Denise had baffled him with her talk of unfaithfulness and her parting comment about the leather suit. He couldn't believe she desired him. The idea that she would risk ruining both their lives for some passing thrill was as appalling as it was improbable.

With a few words and gestures, she had ignited a wildfire that, though he kept pouring cold questions over it—what could she see in him? How could he have so foolishly misunderstood her sisterly affection? Was he allowing himself to be played for a complete fool? Didn't the waiting car suggest the whole encounter had been choreographed to the final stride?—raged on regardless.

Looming largest and most hideously of all was the fear of committing a terrible transgression. Denise herself had seemed to suggest that it wouldn't be like infidelity at all. But would it feel like incest? That was the coldest and most frightening question.

The next morning, he was on his bike, about halfway to the playing fields, when he realised he hadn't changed his Fantasy team. It left a sickening feeling in his gut. He couldn't even remember who was in his team with certainty. He was confused whether a particular player was suspended or whether that had been last week. He'd known exactly who he was going to transfer out, but he hadn't done it. Here he was, after leading the league for eighteen straight Matchdays—about to lose it all on the final day.

He was still fretting when he parked his bike and scanned the vast playing fields filled with short, wide goals and tiny people in red- and green- and mustard-coloured bibs. There must have been a thousand adults there watching or supervising. He was sweating and feeling like the day had lost all its promise when Denise walked out of the crowd with her long straight legs and her long brown hair waving across her shoulders. She was dressed in a tight-fitting leather jacket and trousers.

'How do you like my leathers?' she asked, posing for him. 'Well, what are we standing around for? Are you going to take me for a ride?'

'Where shall we go?' he asked, stupidly.

'Somewhere wonderful.'

She put on the spare helmet and sat behind him. She was holding him tightly around his hips. He edged her wrists up to his chest with his elbows. He drove her out of the suburbs and onto some of his favourite country lanes. He leant the bike over around the bends, thinking it would excite her. When he felt her sliding her hands down to his thighs he slowed right down. He had suddenly become terrified of killing them both in a crash.

They were still a quarter of an hour away from The Rose and Crown, a country pub he'd decided to take her to, when she unzipped his jacket and started rubbing her hands over his chest. He remembered reading a story that Elvis Presley had had an orgasm in his black leather outfit while performing on an American tv show. He had a vision of them being found dead in a hedgerow with her hands still on his breasts and his pants full of semen.

When they dismounted, it seemed inevitable that they would make love. But after they'd sat in the garden and drunk their diet cokes, the moment seemed to have passed. She looked at her watch.

'I hope the twins have got into the next round.'

On the way back, there was a favourite place of his that he liked to stop at and wanted to show her. He'd imagined them having sex there and he liked the idea of taking her there to see it without telling her. They walked through a beech and hawthorn wood under the fresh young lime-coloured canopy, with the may tree blossoms coming out.

'The bluebells are still out!' she exclaimed, delighted. They were spread across the floor of the wood like gauzy carpet. She came very close to him and looked into his face. 'Oh! I'd like so much to make love amongst the bluebells. They smell divine.'

He found himself scanning a mental gallery of his friends, all men, all rivals and adversaries. There were the guys in the pub, the Fantasy League players, those near the top who looked daggers at him over their pints, and those lower down who patted him on the back and waited for him to fall. There were the guys he biked with, the speed merchants with German machines more powerful than his, or those with beautiful old Triumphs or Ducatis, who looked at his Honda with scorn. And some of the old-timers at the Firm were friends, of a sort, having worked together for a decade; still cheating on their expenses, submitting dubious commission statements, making unauthorised purchases, or plaguing him with ageing debtors. The modes of attack and defence were the only ways he'd known as an adult man, and they were what he brought home to Linda and the kids; he lived fully armoured and armed.

And yet he and Denise were co-conspirators, working together with one end in mind; to have sex without being unfaithful, exactly. He felt soft and breathless at the same time, just thinking about her. It was exhilarating to think that they wanted the same thing.

He had imagined that sex with her would seem like a touch from a goddess, a long-limbed, blemish-less satin-sheened Amazonian queen, able to abandon herself to the heat of passion but at the same time be cool to the touch. As he arched up above her, he could only catch a flashing impression of her tanned thighs, spread as far as the leather pants around her shins would allow. Why would a woman who took such care to look beautiful allow him to do this? The whole moment was like a flash, that might have seemed momentous if he'd been able to step back and witness it. He lay against her leather jacket with one hand still under the lime tee-shirt where he'd half undone her bra and pulled it askew.

All the way back he waited for the remorse to kick in. But he felt happy, not just about what they'd done, but about everything. He wondered whether she'd be angry and scornful, but when they dismounted, and she'd taken off her helmet and shaken her hair loose, she ran a finger down his jawline.

'I've got a nettle rash on my bum. How am I going to explain that away?' And she laughed and waved him off.

When Darren came in from his ride, she couldn't help herself.

'New after-shave Dazzler? Bluebells?'

'It must be Denise's perfume.' He said, walking past her without pausing. 'We watched her kids playing football.'

'Did they do well?'

'No idea. They were still at it when I left.'

She was relieved that it was Denise. It irritated her that Denise had a thing for Darren. It was part of

Denise's superiority over Linda that she could see things in Darren that Linda herself was blind to. But Denise wouldn't get mixed up with him, she was sure of that. If Denise ever fooled around, it would be with a man who wore Italian clothes and drove a convertible, or something like that.

She caught him up in the bedroom.

'I hear congratulations are in order.'

'Uh?' Denise had told her about the deal. Darren had never mentioned it. 'Oh, you mean this Singapore business.'

'Of course, I do. Denise said you'd sorted everything out for Robbie.'

'Yeah. It would be better if Robbie didn't leave things so that they always need sorting out.'

'But Dazz, it's wonderful. We can pay off the mortgage and put something aside for school fees for the kids. I'm so proud of you.'

He looked as though he was only just thinking this through for the first time. Too busy obsessing about his bloody Fantasy Football, more than likely. But he smiled and surprised her.

'You're right, Linz. Yeah. It's pretty good isn't it? And we'll have a bit left over to get you a fancy new car. What do you say to that?'

She went up on tiptoe and he let her kiss him. She started unzipping his leathers, but he turned away, as if he was suddenly shy.

'We'll disturb the kids.'

'I got you a present. To say well done—and thank you.'

'Let me shower and I'll be right down.'

When he came into the kitchen, ten minutes later, she sang out, 'Ta-ra!'

The dog was in its crate, pawing at the door. Their oldest, Jessica, held onto the cage trying to poke the dog with her splayed fingers.

Darren stared dumbfounded.

'What the hell is that?'

'It's a dog. A lurcher. The kids and I went and picked him out. He's from an old lady in Loughton who just lost her husband. He's already house-trained.'

Darren had that look about him that he had when he was doing business calculations in his head while pretending to keep up a conversation.

'What am I going to do with a *dog*?'

'Come on Dazzler. Get with the programme. You're going to give it a name. You're going to tickle it under its chin. You're going to buy a carrier for your bike and take it into the office. And first of all, you're going to take it for a walk. Here you go, here's the lead and a bag for the poop. Off you go.'

'Poop?'

He looked all helpless and in need of rescuing, but she had steeled herself against this, and pressed ahead. 'Go on. Twenty minutes. It'll do you good.'

Miraculously, or so it seemed to her, he took the lead from her, attached it to the dog, and led it out of the back door.

'And you're going to take it to the vets to get it neutered,' she called after him. 'I've booked you in for next Saturday morning.'

She knew the final matches of the football season were all being played that afternoon. But Darren was strangely relaxed. He'd been playing with Jess and the dog, trying to come up with a name. It was a beautiful Spring afternoon. She'd put on a flowery dress.

Now Jess was watching a video. The baby was napping. Darren had taken the dog out into the garden. She stood at the kitchen window enjoying the sight of them apparently in animated conversation. She saw Darren reach inside his hip pocket and look at his phone. He sank to his knees on the grass. Linda thought he'd had a seizure; she rushed out to him.

'Grimesy's Captain's been sent off.'

She thought he was going to start crying.

'I've won the League!"

She started laughing and stroking his hair, 'You silly fool. I always knew you would.'

Then she did something they hadn't done since she'd been pregnant with Jess. She lifted her dress over his head and pressed his face against her panties. The dog nuzzled around their feet wondering what had happened to its master.

I don't know where you've been, Dazzler, she thought, but I've got you back now.

She arched her back and dug her nails into his scalp. They toppled over onto the grass and lay next to each other kissing softly.

'Sergio,' he said. 'I'm going to call him Sergio.'

'Is that who got sent off?'

'No. It was the player I forgot to transfer yesterday. My lucky omen.'

His phone rang. He mouthed 'Robbie,' to her. 'From Singapore.'

'Yeah. Hey Robbie, that's great news! Yeah, thanks. Yeah, you too…nice work, Bobbie Dazzler…yeah, I do. I suspect you knew before I did…Sergio he's called. By the way, I just won the Fantasy League. Yeah, I know we were supposed to let the staff win, but *I* won. Dead right I'm gonna celebrate. Get off the phone! I've got a beautiful woman here waiting for me to open the Prosecco. Yeah, love you too.'

And Robbie was gone again.

Rainfall

The phone on Robin's desk, which no one other than his boss in London ever called, started ringing. He had been staring out of the window, contemplating the cloud formations...the way he loved to do on a late Spring day, or any day for that matter. He held the current issue of Climatology Week in one hand. In a single motion, he slid off the windowsill and reached across his desk as if to take a smart catch at extra cover. His boss's name was Harlequin.

'Harley, hello! Good afternoon. Yes, absolutely fine, thanks. What can I do you for?'

Robin received only three types of call from Harley. There were calls about the likely weather on a particular afternoon or evening at Hurlingham or Ascot and whether or not his wife should wear a jacket or shawl. Then there were calls about specific budget items; the question was usually framed as, 'Do you think Licence payers might be just as content without the benefit of your research trip to

Mauritius?' And finally, there were the calls, like this one, that began, 'Now, look, Robin…'

'I've been talking to the Minister…'

(Robin had attended a meeting with Harley and the Minister on one occasion; the meeting when they'd told him they were outsourcing the Meteorology department. Harley had mostly listened and agreed.)

'…and he's got himself into a proper lather…'

'About?'

'This Scottish business, of course. Questions have been asked in the House.'

Robin knew about the questions in the House. He'd drafted the answers.

'Yes, but Harley, we can't do anything about the weather, in Scotland or anywhere else. We've been through this.'

'Now, don't try and get me chasing that red herring again, Robin.'

'It just rains more in Scotland. If the Scottish MPs spent more time there, they wouldn't find it so shocking.'

'Robin, you know as well as I do, it's not the weather they're questioning. It's the forecast.'

'Surely…'

'They think we're anti-Scottish, always forecasting rain.'

Robin had had to go up to London twice to present the analysis, once to the Department and again to a House of Commons Committee. He was passionate about multi-variate regression and had left both groups bamboozled.

'We're not talking about the weather, Robin. This is political. It's about keeping the Scots happy.'

'What, by giving them false weather forecasts?'

'Don't be flippant. They pay their Licence Fee, same as everyone else. The Government's view is that they're entitled to as good a weather forecast as anybody else.'

'We deal in isobars, Harley.'

'It's called *interpretation*, Robin. I'm asking you to give a more favourable *interpretation* for Scotland.'

'Are you expecting us to doctor the charts or just mis-interpret what they say?'

'Don't try to get me embroiled, Robin. I'm giving you direction. You need to sort out the execution with your people.'

'They're not 'our' people anymore.' To be honest, he no longer felt like it was 'his' forecast, either.

'All the better. Make sure the Minister and I can be seen to have had nothing to do with it.'

'What!?'

'Run along, now, Robin; there's a good chap.'

Harley put the phone down. The Minister and an official were standing next to him. 'There, that wasn't so hard,' the official said, smiling at the Minister.

Robin called someone he knew in Compliance, who took a few minutes to check and then told him: No, the call had not been recorded. It had come in from a scrambled source. Robin opened a new folder on his laptop, giving it a short expletive as a code name.

He let things drift for a couple of weeks, then drove down to the West Country, where the company that now employed the meteorologists was headquartered. Across Salisbury Plain he could watch the isobars tighten, the great banks of cumulus and cumulonimbus running up like clippers under full sail from the south-west.

His counterpart down there was Freya, a commercial woman, not a meteorologist. This had seemed to Robin to be the ultimate humiliation after he had navigated the hateful task of outsourcing his department. But for the first time, he now saw that it might prove advantageous. He had always found Freya, who was Czech, and spoke in the clipped phrases of a prison officer, very intimidating. But as he rehearsed in his mind various ways of handling the discussion, he saw how helpful it might be that she neither understood nor cared about either the forecast or the weather in Scotland.

What he had in mind was simply encouraging her to motivate her meteorologists to give a more *upbeat* interpretation of the prospects for Scotland. He'd tried out a few words that seemed most consistent with taxpayers getting what they deserved, and he'd settled on *'upbeat'* and, if absolutely necessary, *'cheerful.'* No-one could get fired for wanting a more *upbeat* forecast. He toyed with the idea of offering a modest bonus for the number of times the words 'dry', 'sun' and even 'fair' were uttered. Perhaps they could start a competition, a kind of ladder, with prizes. She was relatively young, and he thought these ideas would appeal to her.

He didn't think this for very long. She was more freezing fog than sunny spells.

'We are contracted to provide an independent service, as you very well know,' she said, as if to end the discussion barely two minutes in, without so much as the offer of a cup of coffee.

They went around the same argument three times. He heard himself use the same hateful phrases as Harley. 'We're talking about *interpretation*.'

'No,' she fired back, '*You* are talking about interpretation. *I* am talking about our contract, which has nothing to say about interpretation.'

Well, obviously, a contract to do with weather forecasts could hardly have an explicit clause in it that allowed the client to control the interpretation, could it? he wanted to say, but thought better of it. Instead he asked, 'So if it were renegotiated, and such a clause were included?'

'That would be a commercial matter.'

In other words, it would involve a lot of money. His original plan had been to take her out to lunch, but the meeting was over in twenty minutes. He asked if there was somewhere he could work. She suggested the reception area. He asked if there was Wi-Fi. She said she'd heard they had good Wi-Fi in the Starbucks in the town centre. He smiled, 'Of course,' and gave up.

At least he hadn't had time to mention Scotland explicitly before the incoming hail had driven him backwards out of the building and into the car park. Mentally, he started composing an email to Harley weighing up the pros and cons of renegotiating the contract. It was the Friday before the Summer Solstice and he was still thinking over the memo when he reached the tail of a huge queue of traffic on the road past Stonehenge.

While stationary, he could track the pressure dropping on an app on his phone. He placed a bet with himself as to exactly when the rain would arrive. Half an hour later, the ruins finally appeared over the brow of the downs as he counted down the arrival of the rain. Three minutes, two minutes…it hit his rear windscreen eighty-three seconds before he'd forecast. Irritating to get it wrong, but not bad. It had taken so long to get to the monument that it had brightened up again, and he decided he might as well go in and walk around. It was on his second circuit of the stones that an idea came to him. In the contract he had certain rights to select or exclude presenters specifically from appearing on television. This had been intended to protect taxpayers from the dumbing down of the forecast that was thought to be the biggest risk of placing it in commercial hands. There was nothing to stop him turning this on its head, however, to meet his current purposes. He would have to look up the details, but that might be his best way in. A little bit of cheerfulness didn't seem a lot to ask in return for a bit of fame and the chance to appear on The Great British Bake Off or Strictly Come Dancing.

Before he had a chance to take this idea any further, there was a quite unexpected change in the weather. A shift in the jet stream weakened the Atlantic fronts and drew them further North. Starting from the August Bank Holiday, the whole of Scotland from the Western Isles south and east to the Tweed, basked in a glorious Indian summer.

Robin had had a lazy Bank Holiday weekend. Normally he would have spent the Sunday evening running over the raw data, assembling his own charts from scratch, writing up a dozen headlines and catch phrases, ready to judge the presenters on Monday morning. But on this particular Monday morning he was caught completely by surprise. It was Tonya on the breakfast show, (Business and French from Loughborough, but always pleasant enough). He sat bolt upright when he heard her talking airily about, 'several days of settled warm weather', and 'clear night skies' while gesturing to the north and west of

Scotland. By the time Usman, the public's favourite weatherman, came on, Robin had gone over the charts with a fine-toothed comb.

Yes, not only was the forecast for Scotland for several weeks of excellent weather, but it was much more favourable than for anywhere else in the British Isles.

It took Harley till Thursday to catch on. Robin received an email at eight a.m.: *Noticeable improvement, Robin. Has not been lost on the Minister. Keep up the good work.*

Robin started a reply saying that the excellent forecasts had been made considerably easier by the excellent weather, but he thought better of it. He'd had a research sabbatical approved sufficiently long ago that Harley would have forgotten, and he didn't want to give him an excuse to remember. With a bit of luck, he thought, he'd be in the Galapagos before the weather broke in Tobermory.

It was not to be.

He'd risked attracting the Wrath of Freya by writing encouraging notes to the forecasting team direct, but as soon as the unseasonal High pressure had been dislodged and a procession of cold fronts reasserted themselves across the North Atlantic, the forecasts returned to their former grim tone.

Harley called him at home and demanded, 'What the hell is going on, Robin? I thought you had this under control.'

'The weather's got worse, Harley, and following a long-standing but thus far under-researched correlation, so have the weather forecasts.'

'Oh, don't give me excuses. We can't go through another round of this. Someone's going to lose their job, and believe me, the Minister will make damn sure it's not him.'

Robin shared his idea to use the contract to give greater prominence to the more *upbeat* presenters, and gradually remove those that Harley had taken to calling the Socialist Realists.

'You think we can make it stick?' was all he wanted to know.

'Will you back me when we have to take on the difficult cases?'

'As always, Robin. You know that.'

That was all the reassurance Robin was offered. He called a meeting of all the meteorological team who weren't on duty for the following Thursday. He knew everything was going to be okay when Freya called to say she'd got stuck behind an overturned lorry on the A303 and wouldn't make it to the meeting. 'Oh, I'm so terribly sorry,' he managed to say. 'Don't worry. We'll have a debrief over the phone.'

There were about twenty-five people in the room, several of whom he'd worked with for many years. Some were broadcasting presenters with no qualifications; they could just as easily have been reading out the traffic updates on local radio. But there were a few experienced, highly qualified meteorologists, too, like Bernie, Kath and Usman. They respected him. After all, he was the first to have published analysis of the effect of El Nino on the North Atlantic system. They knew he'd been selected to join the Woods Hole South Pacific Climate Monitoring Survey that winter; he'd just got his Chilean visa and was waiting for confirmation of the budget. But they sensed something had gone wrong; that this was not the Robin they had admired and trusted all these years.

He found it hard to maintain eye contact with Usman or Kath and decided to concentrate on some of the junior members who could presumably be relied on to do what they were told. He smiled at Tonya, whom he thought of as his ally, the bringer of sunny skies. And Rolf, who had the extra cachet of a slightly Germanic accent, though, Robin knew, he'd previously been a flight attendant.

'Look,' he began, 'We're all professionals. I don't want to beat about the bush.' This was already enough to start a stir. 'Everyone in the United Kingdom pays the same licence fee,' he made a little gesture to indicate how obviously true this was, 'and yet,' he slowed down to make sure the undeniable logic of what he had to say sank in, 'some people get a much better weather forecast than others.'

More than half the faces looked back at him incredulously. He looked at Tonya and smiled; it just needed one person to say: *you know, when you look at it that way, Robin's right.* But nobody said a thing.

'And, you know,' he was still speaking slowly, emphasising how logical this all was, and how unavoidable the conclusion must be, once he got to it, 'the citizens who pay the licence fee, expect a fair and equal weather forecast, wherever they live. You can't argue with that, can you?'

Usman felt he could argue with that. 'I hear that what you are really talking about is Scotland; you want us to make up better forecasts for Scotland. Is that true?'

'Well, Scotland! There's a terrific example of what I'm talking about, Usman. Could anybody here honestly say that the Scots get as good a forecast as people paying exactly the same fee in East Anglia?'

Bernie shook his head and spoke with apparent irritation, 'But Robin, East Anglia is the driest region in Britain.'

'But you're confusing the weather with the forecast, Bernie. Come on, you're all educated, sophisticated professionals; you know the difference between the territory and the map of the territory.'

It had taken Usman a few minutes to straighten out what Robin meant. 'You are saying you want us to mislead the people in Scotland. You want us to lie to them?'

Robin couldn't help looking over his shoulder to check that no-one else had entered. This was in danger of getting out of hand.

'Now look everyone, that sort of thing is completely out of the question. Good Heavens! Come on, Usman, we're talking here about providing a service; a fair and equal service to all our customers.'

'We're doing the weather forecast, Robin, not valeting cars.'

'Exactly and what I am saying to you is that we have a responsibility to give the public in Scotland a cheerful and upbeat forecast…'

'…regardless of the weather…'

'Yes. Regardless of the weather. More or less.'

There was uproar. Robin caught the eye of Debi a slender, long-legged brunette who looked terrific alongside a map of the British Isles, whom he'd rescued from covering minor sports in Welsh. They exchanged a confederate smile. There were biddable young people in the room, he felt sure.

When things calmed down, Kath asked what she obviously regarded as a trump question. 'What about snow? Is snow cheerful and upbeat?'

There was quiet laughter.

Robin hadn't considered snow, but the answer came to him without any thought. 'Yes, I think the prospect of snow can be reported very cheerfully, especially any time around Christmas.'

'This is preposterous,' Bernie was quite angry now. 'What are you doing Robin?'

This was a question Robin had asked himself many times in recent weeks. The truth was, it just didn't feel like any of this was his business any more. He wanted to be on a boat out on the Southern Ocean taking measurements of temperature and circulation.

Kath joined in. 'You're playing some kind of political game. We're not involved in politics. We're meteorologists.'

He left Kath's hyperbolic comment hanging in the air, losing steam. Maybe half of them could claim to be meteorologists. Debi had a Geography degree from Glamorgan, but he was pretty sure it was Urban Geography, whatever that might be.

Usman, the People's Favourite, unwittingly lit the touch paper. 'What if we don't agree? What if we refuse to distort the forecast? You can't force us to do this. We refuse to condone the politicisation of the weather forecast.'

There was a subdued cheer from the Socialist Realist faction.

Robin put on his saddest face. 'Well, I should remind you that the Minister has the statutory right to replace presenters who are deemed incompetent, unsuitable or irresponsible.'

Some people gasped; others growled. He heard 'You can't!' and 'You won't!' from a few different directions.

'I'm a meteorologist like many of you. I don't want to see the profession at war with the taxpayer. And you know, when you stop and think about it, all we're saying is that if you want to present on the television, you owe it to the taxpayer to put as cheerful and upbeat an interpretation on the forecast as you can. That's not much to ask, is it?' He smiled, making eye contact with those he thought persuadable, one by one. He stood his ground while the meeting broke up around him.

Freya was incandescent when she called him a couple of hours later, having battled her way back to her office. He could tell she was speaking through tightly compressed lips, trying to retain a facade of professionalism. After a dozen dead-bat answers in which he refused to admit even the most self-evident facts from the meeting she finally blew up.

'You are weaponising the contract to eviscerate the service we provide. My company will not stand for it. We will bring you down. I make you a promise.'

'Eviscerate', he thought. Definitely a Bernie word. He wouldn't forget that.

It took about a week for the first press reports to appear. The first reports were jokey in tone. '*Under the*

Weather' was one headline; *'Brighter Skies Forecast'* was another. Then the Times published a piece accusing the Government of political interference in the Weather Forecast. The Government was challenged to assure the public of the integrity of its weather service. The inevitable question was asked in the House. Robin drafted a response starting with a humorous denial that the Government had ever claimed to have any influence over the weather and reminding the Honourable Member that the independence of the weather forecast was written into the contract with the service provider.

The Minister had received polling data that the public liked the idea of more *upbeat* forecasts. It was particularly popular in areas exposed to the Atlantic. Scottish and Welsh MPs were backing it. So, when Freya called up to ask for more explicit assurances that Robin had no intention of executing on his threats to interfere with her roster of presenters, he held the whip hand.

'I expect you and your presenters to get on the front foot, Freya. Then we won't need to speak about it again.'

During November, Robin divided his time between preparing for his trip to the South Pacific and monitoring the performance of the forecasters. He no longer paid any attention to the weather data itself. He had access to the transcripts and had rigged up some software that counted the frequency of various phrases and combinations of words. By the middle of the month he had his Leader Board, with Debi at the top, and Kath and Usman down in the bottom third. He sent congratulatory memos to the top quartile. Bernie sat on the bottom rung. Robin called Freya. He'd done mouth-relaxing exercises for several minutes before dialling. He wanted to ooze composure.

'I'd like to see Bernie spending more time on the radio.'

To her credit, she'd seen it coming. She referred him to the ninety-day formal process. She obviously thought that Robin would never get the Minister to actually write the letter. Robin had taken the precaution of securing the Minister's signature in advance; it was on the letter on the desk in front of him.

'Look Freya, we both want the same thing; *a happy, popular and authoritative* weather *service* and a contract extension without a competitive tender. I'm not sure that a formal process would be consistent with that, would it?' There was what he took to be compliant silence at the other end of the call. 'Let me just tell you who the most and least positive presenters have been so far this month, and you can decide how to adjust accordingly,' he smiled into the phone.

As soon as he'd signed off, he got back to the job of selecting his storm-proof outerwear for the Southern Ocean section of the research trip.

Sure enough, Debi, Tonya and Rolf started to dominate the prime slots. Bernie had disappeared onto local radio somewhere. Usman and Kath refused to get the message. If anything, they dug in, repeatedly insisting that the weather in the north and west would be truly awful. By the end of November, they were propping up Robin's Leader board. He couldn't move against Usman without Harley's backing, and Harley, in turn, took the question of demoting a television weather presenter to the radio to the Right Honourable Minister of State, who refused to give a positive instruction, but did not contradict Harley when he stated his intention to request Usman's removal from the nation's screens.

By this point, Usman was mostly doing late night shifts, and Robin imagined that he'd be secretly pleased to move to daytime radio. This was the tack he took with Freya, anyway.

'This will go down very badly,' she said. No longer was she giving him clipped instructions; now it was mostly complaints. 'The team won't like it. He's popular with the Newsroom. The public trust him.'

'Well, it's your decision, of course,' Robin said, trying to sound menacing—a tone he'd never mastered.

The weather forecasters took Usman's departure in their stride, but the same could not be said of either Usman or the general public. Out of nowhere, Freya started forwarding Robin hundreds of emails and text messages from outraged members of the public demanding Usman's return. The Minister was cornered in the corridors of the House by anxious MPs brandishing angry letters from constituents. Worst of all, Usman went on Breakfast television, not to give the forecast, but sit on the sofa and tell his story. #BringBackOurUsman went viral on Twitter and Facebook. Usman was invited to write an Op-ed piece in the Sunday Times setting out his vision for a truly independent weather forecasting service of undisputed integrity, trusted by all, where forecasters were judged only by the accuracy of their forecasts. The Minister started panicking, summoning Robin and Freya to a crisis meeting in Whitehall. Robin had the Minister's original signed, formal letter, and email confirmation from Harley to seek Usman's removal, to protect him. Freya played a straight bat, never varying from her position that she was conforming to the terms of the contract and that should be that.

The next day the Minister called Robin direct. It was unprecedented. The call lasted less than two minutes. 'Ah yes, Robin, there's a couple of points I wanted to straighten out with you.'

'Yes, Minister.'

'I'd like you to encourage the weather service people to put this Usman chap back on the television. Make sure he does Countryfile this Sunday would you, so the PM sees it.'

'Yes, Minister.'

'And…er…we'll let you know in the next week or so…you'll have a new manager here in the Department. Harley's moved on…something in Farming, I believe.'

'Yes, Minister. Thank you, Minister.'

He was damned if he was going to grovel to bloody Freya. He stared out of the window at a bank of stratocumulus with cumulonimbus building behind it. He didn't care about the British weather anymore to be honest. It felt like somebody else's problem, even if he wasn't sure whose. He'd had confirmation that his papers were in order, his equipment had been procured and his tickets to Lima would be sent to him any day now. He'd written to the most junior person in HR that he thought he could get away with to confirm that he was about to begin his previously approved Sabbatical. He'd remembered to say how much he was looking forward to returning to work the following July.

He and Freya missed each other a few times and it was mid-afternoon before they spoke. He had rehearsed his lines a hundred times by then. He was going to offer Usman a way back into the fold. There was no reason why he should be completely cut off, as long as he was prepared to bend a little. Freya bridled at this. Usman wasn't in a bending frame of mind, she said. Well, Robin insisted, he was prepared to give him a chance and see how it went. He was suddenly afraid that she might call his bluff and demand complete reinstatement. He'd have had to concede, though he'd have despised himself for it. But though Freya was stony and cold, she was also silent. He was able to take the next step.

'What about putting him on Countryfile this Sunday?' he tried to sound like he'd just come up with the idea.

The silence lasted five seconds...ten seconds. His palms were sweating. He wondered whether saying something about bringing the nation's favourites together would seal the deal but saying anything felt too risky.

'Yes, I can probably schedule him in,' she said, as though they were talking about a prison visit.

He thanked her and ended the call and rewarded himself with a triumphant circuit around his desk, pumping his fists and acknowledging the roar of an imaginary crowd.

The following week, a fortnight before Christmas, something magical happened. It started snowing, first in Aberdeenshire, then in Ross and Cromarty and finally all across Scotland and the Borders. Debi and Tonya and someone he'd never seen before called Shane took it upon themselves to wear Christmas jumpers and even Santa hats. While the main News ground out stories of over-turned lorries and starving cattle, the weather forecasters spread delight across Scotland and the North with the promise of closed factories and offices, days off school, sledding and even a White Christmas.

On the Winter Solstice, the Minister called to congratulate him. Robin saw the Unknown Caller signal come up on his phone. He was sitting at gate B35, next to a large decorated tree with a teddy bear dressed as Santa Claus on top, waiting to board his flight to Lima. He declined the call and went back to reading Climatology Week. There was snow forecast for the South East the following day. The Minister might be less happy when it was his car that couldn't get out of the drive. But Robin would be out on the endless, empty South Pacific by then.

Closing the Gap

Throughout the Fall, Mark Horne had been shuttling back and forth between his offices in Menlo Park and Twickenham, visiting the family home in Cobham every second or third weekend. He arrived at Heathrow on Christmas morning. He found something comforting about the fact that for airports and the airlines, every day was the same. Christmas Eve meant nothing in California. He put this down to the lack of Scandinavian influence; the westward spread of the Norse petering out in Minnesota, having found everything they wanted. The Christmas work ethic appealed to his sense of being a spear-bearer in the front rank of the phalanx, absorbing the full brunt of the World's indifference.

His wife, Melissa, was standing on the front steps when the taxi swung into the driveway. This was her most despicable trick; it would take forty-eight hours to bring her down to the moral lowlands in which they both belonged.

'Oh, Darling,' she said so that the taxi driver could hear, turning away decisively so as to avoid any contact with his lips. His phone was buzzing in his back pocket. 'How is your APO?' she asked.

'IPO,' he corrected her. They'd had this exchange a dozen times before. He'd done this trick more than once; steering a company to its Initial Public Offering. He was hired specifically to perform the feat of bringing a fragile but fast-growing company to the public markets. His current company was scheduled to list on the Nasdaq in the Spring, buoyed up by the seemingly limitless, never-ending bull market and a surge in sales the previous summer.

Melissa led him into the house, holding the secret that she had bought him the perfect present. It was not that they had fights, or even that they hated each other. It was more that they each lived at the extreme margins of each other's lives. Could it really be true that they lived in a spherical world so that the further they drifted apart the more inevitably they ended up together?

One thing her father had impressed into her character was that the ideal man does the looking after and needs none in return. She'd looked for that in every boyfriend until she'd finally found it in Mark. It was a rare, but characteristic, concession that she'd put wrapping paper next to his shaving bag so he could wrap whatever he had bought her at the airport.

Her sister was coming for lunch with her socialist revolutionary husband. Actually, Mark rather admired Frank, a hard worker, a good organiser, dead honest. If only he'd applied his talents to something more productive than the Militant Tendency, or whatever it was called these days, he might have been able to get a man to drive them out to Cobham instead of taking the train from Waterloo, or send his bright children to a decent school, or pay for his wife's cancer treatment. Mel was paying for that. She had a big heart, but only for the halt and the lame. Would she care for him more when he couldn't lift his slippers above the carpet pile or remember what he'd said five minutes ago?

'Go on. You'd better answer it,' she said.

'It's not a call,' he said, but he took the phone out anyhow.

It was two o'clock in the morning in California. It was a text message from the Vice President of Sales. *Stretch update—increasing the risk factor to point-two.*

'Shit!' he exclaimed, and then, 'Oh! Sorry, Darling.' On Christmas fucking Day, though! What a useless fucking bastard. A twenty percent shortfall in sales—and to call it a 'risk' with six days to go before the end of the year. The phone buzzed again: *Don't worry. The U.S. works right through to the New Year.* What a load of bollocks. He tapped his reply. *Go to bed and wake up with some better news.* He thought about wishing the guy's kids a merry Christmas, but actually he wished they would wake up with an incurable disease.

'Go up and shower and shave,' she said.

She knew how pleased and resentful he'd feel when he saw that she'd bought a present from him for their daughter. 'I'll see if Candy's getting up.' She gave him a gentle push up the stairs.

She went into the back of the house and sat down on the edge of the sofa in the TV room. Candy had fallen asleep in a heap, watching a *Fast and Furious* movie. Her boyfriend Eric, who was slowly but steadily filling various galleries in east London with unsold art works, was away at a show in Hamburg where something from his Outrage series was being shown. When Mel had come down for breakfast she'd draped a down jacket over her, but it had slipped onto the floor. She stroked the white-blonde halo of hair, conjuring images of her daughter as a three-year-old fairy-shepherd, singing in the kindergarten Christmas show, methodically and seriously stepping through her little routine, or as Dick Whittington's cat, in junior school, curled up with her tail held over her shoulder.

Mark had felt so pleased with himself that he'd remembered to get a present for Mel at the airport. He'd been thinking that he'd have to resort to perfume, but they'd had one Moncler ski jacket in her size in a colour he knew she'd like. But he'd forgotten that Candy would be home. God why was everything so hard? After he'd showered, he picked up his shaving kit and found the wrapping paper and the cashmere sweater wrapped in silver paper. His first thought was that his wonderful wife had rescued him from catastrophe. But then he peeked inside the paper and saw that the sweater was a colour that might be called 'Pink Frost' and he realised that he'd been set up. She must have thought he wouldn't bother to look. Jesus! He'd be better off heading out to the Paki-store and getting her a bottle of Southern Comfort.

Melissa's younger sister had been christened Stella-Maria and this summed up the central problem of her life: was she a Stella or a Maria? Instead of going to

University, wild Stella had left home to live in squats with an ever-changing cast of artists, musicians and drug addicts. She refused to have any contact with the global banking system, so Papy David had had to fly over from the Dordogne every few weeks to hand over a fistful of local currency, usually in a Brick Lane curry house. The suits in which he hugged his unbathed daughter and mopped up his Jalfrezi sauce were placed in black rubbish bags and left in the waste basket in his hotel room. Maman Tina had suffered an anxious few years; no contact with her daughter, and the mysterious disappearance of her husband's suits after trips to London that had no apparent purpose. And then Maria had reappeared without warning; with a child on her hip and another in her belly, and a heavily bearded and slightly pot-bellied Frank in tow. Now Tina called her Maria-my-baby, and Papy David called her My Maria of the Wine Dark Sea.

Mark lay on the bed with the towel loosely wrapped around his waist. He hoped Mel might come up and offer to give him a backrub. His phone rang. He knew who it would be; his Chief Executive, Walter, who never slept.

'Good Morning, Walter. Happy Christmas.'

'Have you seen Ronny's Stretch report? It is a bit of a stretch, I know, but then that's why I stretched the budget to bring you on board, Mark.' Walter thought he was being amusing.

'It's not so much a stretch as a gap, Walter. There's six days to go. I can't produce a painting out of a pile of horseshit.'

'I'm sure it's been done before,' said Walter. 'We'll close the gap. But then you'll have to work some magic.'

Mark had to be careful. Walter was the kind of guy who wouldn't think twice about conjuring up a few dubious orders that would age on Mark's balance sheet like unwashed socks in the corner of a drawer. By the time the investors were in due diligence a sales shortfall would have been transformed into a financial control failure.

'I'm sure you'll all do what you can, and you can be sure I'll do what I can.'

'I'm counting on you, Mark, my man.' He could feel Walter beaming across the time zones. 'We all are.'

'Of course, Walter,' said Mark, falling back on his internationally admired ironic deference.

Immediately, he called Astrid, the Danish head of Europe. He wanted to know how much of Ronny's gap came from Europe.

'It's Christmas Day, Mark. I'm not working today.'

'Don't fuck me around, Astrid. You do your stuff on Christmas Eve.'

'No, we are all Americanised, now.'

'Bollocks. Anyway, consider it repayment for your Christmas Day raid on King Alfred.' He was deadpan and she wasn't sure whether he was joking.

'What do you want, Mark?'

'Ronny's just issued a twenty percent stretch warning; with six fucking days to go, Astrid. How much of that is down to you?'

'Can't we talk about this tomorrow? My family is sitting down to our meal.'

'How much?'

'We'll make our number. Now, do you have what you wanted?'

'Is the big postal deal in yet?'

'We'll bring it in. I told you, we'll make our number.'

'How much is it worth? If it doesn't come in, how far short will you be?'

'Mark, will you give yourself a break and enjoy your Christmas Day at home? I told you we'll make our number.'

'How far short—how far short will you be if it doesn't come in?'

'I don't know; about twenty percent.'

'Thank you. Have a great day, Astrid.'

So, Ronny had already given up on the postal deal. That would account for about a third of the gap. Mark was already constructing the slide set he would have to deliver to the analysts in January. He'd built in about seven per cent cushion, had made some unbudgeted cost savings, and currency movements had given him a little boost; so he was thinking he might be presenting a ten per cent shortfall.

Mel sat on the side of the bed.

'You've put on weight.' She pinched his waist and pulled a face. 'You've been drinking too much.'

He looked down towards his belly, but this only caused his jowls to roll up over his jaw.

'Yeah, you're right,' he said. He was drinking too much. 'I saw you got a sweater for me to give to Candy. Thanks. Do you think she'll like it?'

'Oh, it's so "now!" She'll never take it off.'

She could tell he wasn't convinced. She'd bought a sweater for Frank, too, in purple. She was worried that it was the colour of a political party—not Frank's—but it was too late now. In fact, she'd bought an extra-large as well, because with Frank you could never tell from one visit to the next.

'Stella and Frank will be here any minute. Get yourself dressed.' She slapped his thigh.

He pulled his towel off, but she had turned away and walked out of the room.

As soon as she saw Frank, she was pleased she'd bought the extra-large. She never really understood how someone who did nothing that to her mind resembled work could be so permanently stressed.

'Problems with the Centre,' he said.

Stella never held back. 'Poor old Frank's spent the last twenty years tacking to the Centre, only to be attacked by radical types who weren't born when Frank was expelled from the Socialist Workers for advocating Unrestricted Warfare on Global Capital.'

'Yeah. UWGC! Those were the days.'

'Well you're both looking fantastic. Stella must be taking fantastic care of you Frank.'

Frank started to explain that he wasn't doing as well as all that. On the surface, Frank had looked like the kind of man who would take care of wayward Stella, when she'd first moved in with him. But Maria, once she'd come to the fore, had taken a different lesson from their father; to exercise arbitrary and unlimited power within the family unit, and Frank, brought up to be reasonable and accommodating, had duly submitted, just as, outside the home, he'd done to the Party. Beneath her make-up, Stella looked grey from the effort.

'Talking about fantastic, something smells out of this World.' Frank perked up.

'Goose.'

'The ultimate symbol of the alienated worker! Let's hope the *ressentiment* hasn't got into the dark meat, heh?' Stella tried to sound chirpy, but she looked so tired. Her eyes drooped, as though the cancer had eaten away her resistance to gravity.

'I like goose at Christmas,' said Frank.

When Mark walked in Mel was struck by how handsome he still was. He had put on a navy suit and white linen shirt with a navy paisley design inside the collar. He walked with a light spring in his knees and an easy swing of the arms. He smelled terrific, too, as he bent over her to receive a near-miss of a kiss. She hoped he'd bought her something absurdly expensive.

Candy rushed in and gave her aunt a huge hug. There was a great deal of squealing. On her points she reached around Frank and let her cheek brush his. She seemed to have forgotten that she hadn't greeted her father yet.

Mel ushered them into the cavernous dining room with the minstrel gallery. It was impossible to heat, and she'd had a procession of hot water bottles warming the chair seats all morning.

Stella was asking Candy about Eric. She'd seen he'd had a painting in a show in a gallery in Hoxton. 'Sooo trendy,' she said, as if this placed him in a stratum far above the rubbish in the Tate.

'He hasn't sold so much as a dribble all year,' Mark couldn't resist saying. It was a fact.

'Neither did Rothko—for years,' Candy shot back.

After his last big flotation, Mark had bought her a small, unfinished Rothko mythomorphic painting from the forties for a large six figure sum, to reward her for passing her A-levels. He knew nothing about painting and had bought it on the recommendation of an accountant he'd met the day before, but Candy had been thrilled. Now they held each other's gaze.

Most of the time he was in the same room as his daughter he wanted to ask: *Why don't you just get a job?*

He could tell she knew he was thinking this; she could read his mind. The beginning of a smile touched one corner of her lips; she knew he was thinking: *it would solve all your problems.* And she was thinking: *why would I get a job when I can do anything I want, and Eric loves me, and Mummy loves me, and Daddy lets me?*

Halfway through the goose, the doorbell rang. Mark rubbed the grease from his fingers onto his cream-coloured napkin as he went to answer it. It was Papy David and Maman Tina. They were not supposed to come until the following morning.

'Surprise!' Papy David bellowed. 'Merry Christmas everyone.'

He looked awful. Tina looked watchful, as she always did, only more so. Suddenly the hall was full of his daughters and granddaughter shouting and crying and throwing their arms around each other.

Papy David caught Mark by the elbow: 'Go out and bring the gifts in from the car, would you? There's a good fellow.'

He was glad to have the excuse to get away from the melee. It was chilly in the driveway, but the sun was out and it felt good. The driver was standing by the boot as though he'd been expecting him. His name was Toby. Mark asked if he'd like to come in, have a cup of tea and watch television while he waited, but he preferred to wait in the car. Mark found himself envying Toby, driving his smooth powerful BMW around all day, watching movies or snoozing in the reclined front seat between jobs, making the occasional routing decision but otherwise at Fate's beck and call. After he'd put the small bags with the names of obscure Gascon boutiques in the hall, he wandered round to the back of the house to run his hands over the racing lines of his own beautiful DB7 that he never got to drive anymore.

Papy David had always treated Christmas as his personal property; in his soliloquising Mark always pronounced the name like the statue or the painter. He found that amusing. David and Tina came over to London on Christmas Eve, stayed at the Savoy over Christmas and came to see Mel and Candy on Boxing Day morning. The whole holiday revolved around this visit. Present opening was delayed and for days ahead everything was subordinated to Papy's future comfort and convenience. Once, they had arrived with a whole roast turkey fresh from the Savoy's kitchen, waving all Mel's preparations into the composting bucket. Another time they had brought a live tree with a box of baubles and the afternoon had been spent taking down the Hornes' tree and erecting Papy David's in its place. Mark's decision to work through Christmas Eve and take the nine o'clock flight back rather than the seven o'clock or even the five o'clock was in large part an attempt to assert if not his primacy at least his independence. Christmas was always about Waiting for Papy. This year Mark had made sure they'd had to wait for him, or at least Mel had. 'It's a normal working day on the West Coast,' he'd been ready to say...if she'd asked.

He got back to a scene of biblical weeping in the living room. The women were all red eyed and tear stained. Candy was draped over Papy's shoulder crying into his chest. She looked up at Mark as though Papy were a jowly old dog about to be put down. Stella was whimpering, holding Frank's hand tightly. Tina looked on, shedding tears silently, her bird-like face making small pecking motions, always on guard against what might happen next. This was her chosen strategy for living for so long with so unpredictable a man.

Mel sat alone on a sofa, a handkerchief scrunched up in her hand, rocking slightly, staring at an arabesque in the rug, working her lower lip between a pair of canines.

'Pancreas,' Papy said as though the rest of the story was already known. 'Got up into my kidneys and lungs. A matter of weeks, they said.' Tina gave out a sudden sob. Candy unwrapped herself and fled the room. 'Presents!' Papy called after her. 'We must open the presents.'

Bringing the presents out from under the tree and starting the unwrapping restored some sense of normality. Everyone knew what to do. The gifts from Le Sud-Ouest were fabulous and had obviously been chosen with extra care.

'I've had a good run,' David said, very calmly, to Mark as they watched Frank unwrap his sweater. He looked imposing and shrunken at the same time, as though the space around him hadn't fully adjusted to his diminishing condition. 'They say it will be quick,' he nodded as though he were talking about having a tooth pulled. For a moment, Mark admired him.

Stella was thrilled with Frank's purple sweater. Mel was pleased. Perhaps the day would be saved after all. Her first thought when her father had announced his imminent death was that it was no longer possible to give Mark her gift. She had bought him a sky dive and written in the gift card: *Hope you love my death-defying gift.* Then she'd remembered the second purple sweater, and that was what Mark was now opening.

'Oh my God!' Stella squealed. 'Another purple sweater!'

Mark gave her a basilisk-like look over the top of the V-neck. In the moment of silence, Candy toddled into the room on her tip toes dressed in a tutu. There was a pause when they all looked at her with incomprehension. Mel couldn't think where she'd got the tutu from. Then Candy started singing Twinkle, Twinkle Little Star, precisely reproducing the steps and gestures from her first Christmas performance at nursery school. Now, it was Papy David's turn to weep, big tears of happiness and a sweet smile on his face. It only lasted a minute. As one they burst into applause at the end. Mark had been captivated, the critical voice in his head entirely drowned out. He pulled Candy's head down and kissed the crown of her head.

'That was perfect,' he murmured.

'Time to go,' Papy David announced. 'This has been my best Christmas ever!' He beamed around the room. 'My darling Maria, would you like a lift into town?'

It was true, Stella looked like if she weren't carried off, she would be swept away like a fallen leaf.

'Yes, that would be nice,' she said, to no-one in particular.

'Oh! And I'm coming too!' Candy exclaimed. 'I'll open my presents in the car. Then, you can take me to dinner.'

'Well, they won't let you in the Grill Room in that outfit,' Mel laughed.

Candy ran off to change. Five passengers wouldn't fit in Toby's car. There was a debate amongst the women about who should drop out. At one point, poor old Frank was going to go back on the train on his own. Mark and David gazed into each other's eyes, weighing each other up. Then Mark went out to the driveway, unrolled seven twenty-pound notes, pressed them into Toby's hand and told him he could go home. He called his regular driver and asked him to bring the seven-seater over. He took out Candy's unopened presents, stealthily sliding the pink sweater in its silver paper back under the staircase. A few minutes later, he was helping Papy David up into the front seat, and lifting Candy by the waist into the back, with a kiss. Everyone was smiling. Maman Tina was looking on, full of anxiety, but also beaming.

As Mark stood and waved them off, he was thinking of a table on slide seven of his Analyst Deck. This was a crucial slide, one where he would have to close whatever gap Ronny had left for him. He was sure Walter would call again that evening and he wanted to be on the front foot with the skeleton of a story.

Mel slipped her arm inside his. She thought he deserved that. He'd dealt with things beautifully. Her father wanted to go back to France to die. It was so inconsiderate. And then he wanted to be brought back to England to be buried, at the family's old church at Ginverling, that none of them had been to in forty years. He'd arranged nothing, made no preparations. She felt utterly depleted just thinking about it.

They held hands as they walked back into the house.

'And what is that purple sweater all about? Dressing me up like Tweedledee to Frank's fucking Tweedle-plum.'

Mel started giggling and couldn't stop '...sky dive' she gasped, 'defiance of death...couldn't give it...Dad's big announcement...Frank's back-up...'

She was doubled over in the hallway gasping for breath and then disintegrating back into laughter.

Mark started laughing, too, though he wasn't sure what about exactly.

They leant into each other, shaking, until they flopped down on the sofa. She put on an episode of a box set she'd been watching while he was away and nestled her head on his chest and shoulder. She realised he was stroking her breast. She had been determined not to make love, but now it didn't seem such a terrible idea. She would have liked a glass of something bubbly but didn't want him to move. He dropped his cheek onto her head. He'd been thinking about slide twelve, figuring out how to minimise the impact on the forecast for the following quarter. But now, for the first time in more than forty hours, he was asleep, in a deep, dreamless sleep.

The Abuser

Four uniformed officers rang the front doorbell at five in the morning. They'd arrived in two cars, waking David and Sandra when they'd activated the security at the driveway gate. Dave answered the door in a sweatshirt hastily pulled over his pyjamas. He assumed there'd been a break-in somewhere along the road during the night. It happened sometimes. It was only now that he realised it was still dark. He thought it must be something more serious and wondered whether he should have got dressed.

'Good morning. Can I help you?'

'Yes, good morning, sir,' one of the officers stepped forward, introduced himself and confirmed David's identity. 'Sir, I have to ask you to come down to the Station with me. We'd like to ask you some questions.'

'About what?' He had been half-asleep, but now he was breathing sharply, fully alert; it was as though the oxygen masks had dropped.

'You and your wife should get dressed.' There was no pretence at friendliness. The officer was an official with a job to do—to get Mr and Mrs Hooke to the police station with minimum drama.

He didn't know how to explain what was happening to Sandra. She wanted to know what she should pack for him. Did he have time to brush his teeth? Would he need a razor?

When they walked downstairs, the hallway was full of people in white boiler suits and blue disposable gloves.

The Officer stepped forward again.

'I have a warrant to search your house and remove any documents or computer hardware we discover.'

'Am I being accused of something?' David asked.

The police officer was going through an explanation of the search procedure. Neither of them was listening to the other, until the officer looked at them and asked them whether they were ready to leave. Both of them.

Bewildered, they were led by their elbows down the front steps.

Sandy asked no-one in particular, 'Are we being arrested?'

Sandy was the absolute ruler of their home, but the front steps were her boundary; beyond that she leant on Dave's arm and followed his lead. She looked at him now with huge frightened eyes. She hadn't had time to put on any make-up.

They were separated and taken to different cars. A woman officer accompanied Sandra. They exchanged a last frightened look as their heads were ducked into the back seats of their respective vehicles. It occurred to David that he might never see her again. He stared out of the window, racking his brains; what could this be about? Since he'd retired, the most controversial thing he was involved in was the duplicate bridge club in the next town. It suddenly occurred to him that maybe it was something Sandy had done; but what on earth could it be? She power-walked with a neighbour each morning and did Pilates twice a week. Other than that, they spent their days together. They'd just got back from a holiday in Vietnam. Could something have happened there, without them realising?

He was led into a small grey-painted room and sat behind a metal table. He was a sixty-five-year-old man, guilty of a thousand things, but none, so far as he could recall, of any concern to the police. He sat on his own with the swirling memories of humiliations, misjudgements and false steps. For some reason he was certain some senior officer would arrive and straighten things out. After twenty minutes or so, sure enough two men in grey suits entered and sat opposite him. A uniformed officer stood behind them. They introduced themselves as DI this and DS that. They established that it was okay to call him Dave. They passed business cards across the table. Dave wondered whether it was expected that he would have brought cards.

'I'm retired,' he said, lamely. 'Can you tell me what this is about?' he asked trying to sound like a fellow reasonable and intelligent man.

They looked at him as though to say, *you know very well why you're here.*

'I really have no idea what you'd want to talk to me about,' he said, knowing as he said it that it was weak. They looked at him as if to say, *you would say that, wouldn't you*?

'And my wife; why are you talking to my wife?'

'We need to hear her version of events,' the detective on the left said.

Dave glanced down and saw his name was Waters or possibly Walters. Definitely Frank, though; he wondered whether he should call him Frank.

'Events?' Dave asked. 'Are we being accused of something? Should we have a solicitor with us?'

'Do you have anything to hide?' Frank asked. He was obviously the nasty one. 'If you do, then you should call your solicitor.'

Dave's solicitor did house conveyancing and Wills. He'd probably never been inside a police station.

The other detective was called Roger Rockley. He was from the West Country and spoke in a slow drawl. He opened a clipboard and started working through a long list of factual questions to which Dave answered 'Yes' or 'That's right' or 'Correct.' Rockley spoke in a friendly enough tone. He had thick lips and crooked teeth and many suspects must have been tempted to think they could run rings round him.

Roger started asking him questions about a logistics manager at his old firm called Barry Townley. He'd been arrested on suspicion of sexually abusing female employees amongst the warehouse racking. Waves of happiness flooded Dave's bloodstream. He had to restrain himself from reaching across the table and shaking their hands. It wasn't about him at all. It was about some bloke he hardly knew down in the warehouse.

The two detectives remained stony-faced. They wanted to know whether he or any of the other Directors had known of or suspected Mr Townley's alleged activities. They kept asking him whether the Directors had turned a blind eye or covered up what they knew. They said they found it hard to believe that this kind of thing could be going on without the Directors' knowledge. Was there a culture of casual abuse of female employees at the firm? They reminded him that abusive culture started at the top. They kept coming back to the question of whether any of his fellow Directors had been involved in inappropriate relations with employees.

Of course, Ray Mahoney, the big boss, had had a series of young secretaries go through his office. He would take them out for Awaydays and long lunches and to overseas conferences, leaving Amanda, his war-horse of a PA to cover his absence. It had been going on for years when Dave arrived, and by the time he was made a Director, Ray had been through four or five of them. Dave had asked one of them to dinner when they bumped into each other coming out of the toilets at the pub after work. It was an awkward moment and he'd rather blurted it out. He'd lain awake for many nights torturing himself with endless replays of her gesture of rejection.

Did he feel the Directors had fulfilled their responsibilities to protect their staff from predatory behaviour? Frank leant across the table again as if to prod him in the chest.

'Well,' he tried to strike the right balance, 'Obviously, I'm very upset to hear about these allegations, but to be honest, we were a very happy crowd. We all got on so well.'

There was a long silence. Frank looked at him with contempt. Roger peered at him over his reading glasses with his tired, sympathetic eyes, as if to say, *what a feeble man you are without your Director's office and company Jaguar.*

'I need to ask you some questions about your relationship with Miss Hampden,' Roger said in his soft drawl.

'What? Oh, you mean Sandy. She's my wife.'

They asked a lot of detailed questions about the chronology of their relationship to which he answered, 'I don't remember' or 'possibly' or 'it was a long time ago.' Once, when he couldn't recall the answer, he said, 'You'd have to ask Sandy,' and this got him wondering what their colleagues were asking her and what she might be telling them.

'Did you think it was appropriate for you to seduce a junior employee? She was...er...how many years younger than you?'

'Twelve. It's never made any difference.' They must be in a similar awful interrogation room, trying to persuade her that he had abused her, trying to reduce her to tears.

'Really, Dave? You don't think it makes a difference to her, a young woman being put under pressure to start a relationship by her boss's boss, an older man with a Jaguar and beautiful detached house.'

It was true that he'd waited till he had a reason to give her a lift in the Jag to ask her out. He'd been rehearsing different lines for weeks beforehand. He'd fully expected her to turn him down; Ray's secretary hadn't said a word, just pulled a face and made a dismissive gesture with her hand. He'd figured the Jag might impress her, and at least if they were moving she'd have to hear him out. And he'd have an extra few seconds to excuse himself if she reacted badly.

'We were very much in love.'

'It didn't ever occur to you, Dave, that you might be taking advantage of her. Abusing your position of power. You're a big man, Dave. You didn't ever worry that you might be intimidating her?'

It was true she'd called him her Goliath, which he didn't think was such a great nickname. She'd hold onto his arm in her heels, but she had a way of slipping out of his grasp when he held her too tightly. He thought people of her age might move to having sex almost immediately, but somehow a couple of months went by before she stayed late enough that it seemed natural to pull her down onto the sofa and run his hands up her thighs. That was another night he'd lain awake; wondering whether she'd enjoyed it. They hadn't talked about it when he'd driven her home.

'Would you say you'd ever forced yourself on Ms Hampden?' Frank asked leaning forward.

'We've been married almost twenty-five years.' He half-shrugged and opened his arms slightly, inviting them to agree that this was all madness. 'We have two grown-up children. We're a very happy family.'

Frank gazed at him hard, affecting not to have heard a word he'd said. 'Against her will?'

He remembered an awful night when she was pregnant with their youngest when he'd very inexpertly attempted to bugger her. Later she'd told him how much she'd hated it. He felt the guilt on his face; it must have been obvious to the detectives. But there was no way she'd mention it.

'No. Certainly not.'

'Never any violence? Not even the threat of violence in your sexual relations with Ms Hampden?'

There was that phase when she'd wanted him to slap her; she'd lie face down and pretend to squeal until he smacked her on the hips and buttocks. It had made him feel sick, but when she'd demanded that he hit her harder, he hadn't stopped. Once, by the time he'd finished her buttocks were the colour of raw bacon. He'd lain awake imagining what would happen to him if she'd had to go to the Doctor or been spotted changing at the gym. It went on for a few weeks. Then she got pregnant—with their first.

Did they know all this? he wondered. Had Sandy already told them everything? Was that what they kept referring to on their clipboards? Once she'd tried to leave him. He'd found her at the bus stop, for God's sake. He'd thrown her over his shoulder and carried her home, kicking him and punching him, and locked her in the spare room till she calmed down. Just for a moment he thought he might be better off confessing every shameful episode of his life and throwing himself at their mercy.

He heard himself say, 'What do you want me to tell you?' For a moment, he felt heavy and just wanted to be carried out, anywhere.

'What is it you want to tell us?' asked Roger, with a reassuring smile.

He wondered how long it would have taken Sandy to reach this point; of telling them what they wanted. He pulled himself up straight. They wanted to construct a pyramid of little facts that they could build up into a monument to his abuse of a vulnerable woman. But to him, their relationship was a precious, happy and improbable story, and that was the overriding truth to which the facts were servants. That was what he really wanted to say. Once that logic was overturned, any atrocity became possible. Had Sandy managed to hold it together? he wondered.

'I'm wondering whether you feel you might have had sex with the then Ms Hampden, without fully having her consent. What do you think, Dave?'

Without any firm intention, he stood up and slapped his hands on the metal table-top.

'You've gone too far. I'm not going to take any more of this.'

They looked across at him with exactly the same bored expressions, as if they were thinking they'd seen this act a hundred times before. Dave took a couple of breaths and calmed himself down.

'You should charge me or let me go.'

They didn't react. They looked as though they thought they could continue to do neither of those things indefinitely.

'I want to call my solicitor.' He felt as though his lip might start trembling.

Roger pushed his notepad away from him, raised himself wearily to his feet and nodded slowly at Dave.

'Well, if you feel that way,' he said, as if nothing Dave could have done would have been a greater disappointment to him.

They picked up their pens, clipboards and briefcases in slow motion as though to give him every opportunity to reconsider.

Dave thought his knees might give way. He was about to sit down again when they spun around in unison and walked out. He sat with his head bowed, recovering his breath, waiting for someone to bring him a phone. After about twenty minutes, Frank returned with a receipt for whatever they'd taken out of the house, which he signed without reading.

'You are free to go. We'll let you know whether we decide to pursue the case further.'

'What case?'

Frank looked at him as if to say, *you don't give up, do you?*

'How do we get home?' Dave managed to ask, but Frank had already turned his back and walked out, leaving Dave to be ushered through the door by the mute uniformed officer.

Sandy was sitting on a small bench with foam spilling out from its torn seat. She jumped up and ran to hug him. She started sobbing against his shoulder.

'Oh! Honey,' he said, suddenly happy. They hadn't turned her against him.

'I'm so sorry,' she blubbered into his neck, which made him anxious again.

He called for a taxi and asked for a seven- seater. He couldn't face the prospect of chit-chat with the driver. He sat in the corner of the back seat and stared out of the window, the day's events churning over in his mind. After a minute, she came close to him and put her head against his chest.

'I'm so sorry,' she said again.

He flared up, 'What? What are you so sorry about?'

'Don't get angry, darling. I just…I just…told them the truth.'

'What? What truth? What are you talking about? You didn't tell them about the slapping. The slapping was your idea. I hated doing it.'

'What slapping? What do you mean?'

'The slapping. You know.'

'I don't remember any slapping.'

'Oh my God.'

'It must have been with someone before me.'

There never had been anyone else. 'No. It was…oh it doesn't matter. So what did you tell them?'

'About the time you pushed me into that coat cupboard at the office.'

'Come on. It was an office party. And we were going out together by then.'

'You squeezed my breasts and put your hand over my mouth so that I could hardly breath. Oh I hope I haven't got you into too much trouble, darling.'

'Is that it?' If that was the worst… surely no-one could be prosecuted for that. 'Was there anything else?'

'They asked me if I was afraid of you, you know at the beginning. They asked me if I'd been afraid of losing my job if I didn't, you know, go with you.'

He attempted a little chuckle.

'But that's ridiculous. You know I was in awe of you then, as I am now.' He stroked her cheek along the jawline. 'If you'd brushed me off like a crumb it would only have confirmed my view of your superiority. I'd have probably promoted you and given you a raise.' There was a pause. 'So, what did you say?'

'Well, I told them the truth; that yes, I had been a little afraid.'

'Oh my God.'

'You were so powerful at work, darling, so decisive, so different to…afterwards.'

She stretched up and kissed him on the lips.

'I wasn't sure I'd ever get out of there.' Everything he'd felt during the day, the fear, the anger, bafflement, self-hatred and now love for his wife resurged through him. He stifled a sob.

'How long were you waiting there?'

'A couple of hours.'

'What? Why didn't you go home?'

'I wasn't leaving without you, darling.' She looked up again and this time he lowered his lips to hers. 'One thing I realised in there,' she said very quietly, 'was how much I love you. Always have. Still do.'

He kissed her and squeezed her hard.

'Oh am I hurting you?'

'Carry me up to bed and see if you can squeeze the breath out of me.'

He paid the driver and waved him off while Sandy opened the door. Then he picked her up in his arms and carried her into the house and up the stairs.

The Fall

He'd been half-dreaming about the storm when they were woken by a pine branch crashing against their bedroom window. No damage was done, but he had been startled. After he'd laid back down and switched out his reading light, his heart was still racing.

'Work for you to do in the morning,' Mary muttered before she fell back asleep.

He lay in the dark imagining how it would have been to live as a cave-dweller on a night like this. Then his cave was under the sea, everything swaying this way and that, the gale still raging underwater. A giant sea-branch flew past him. A freckled lobster—it spoke in Mary's voice, but he couldn't make out what it was saying—hung before his face, its protuberant eyes adjusting to keep him in focus as it shook its head slowly back and forth. He was cold, chilled all down his right side. He was now on a sailing vessel, sea water pouring across the deck, his face covered in spray so that he could hardly see. The mast cracked behind him and the sails were falling down in a great snapping darkness when he woke up, shivering, half out of his bed sheets.

He opened the bedroom door and Mary's little terrier, Maisie, scampered in and leapt up to snuggle against her breast. To the extent that Maisie could be thought to be property she was jointly owned, but she had a way of letting it be known to whom she belonged. He would have liked to give Maisie a tickle under the chin, but the two of them were already snoring lightly.

He had particular pairs of trousers and boots he liked to wear for garden work and a golf cap from Sanibel to keep sharp twigs away from his eyes. He walked out to the front of the house, as he did early every day to take in the view and give a silent prayer of thanks to the sun or just as often to the rain. When his work had brought him to North Carolina, twenty years ago, he'd had no idea he would find such contentment amidst these rugged, thickly forested mountains. Right on cue, the coyote he saw each morning came trotting around the hairpin below the house and stopped in the road to look at him, as it always did, with its head dropped to one side. Surely it must recognise him, but it gave no sign. Day after day he nodded or waved a greeting to it but had received only baleful indifference in return. They stood about thirty yards apart like this for maybe a minute each morning before the coyote resumed its lope, along the far side of the road, swivelling its head so that it never lost eye contact, on its way to check out the Cramptons' trash further up the hill. These were, he often thought, the most wonderful moments of the day.

He walked round to the back of the house, where the pine branch lay on the patio beneath their bedroom window. It was as long as he was tall. A couple of long thin holly branches had fallen into the box hedge. They were easy enough to pull out and drag to the fire pit at the far end of the yard. The grass was strewn with fans of conifer branches of every size from smaller than his own hand to the size of their breakfast table. The wind was still gusting strongly, brushing smaller debris across the lawn. He thought he should have had breakfast before he started work—a cup of coffee, at least—but there was so much for him to get done.

Across the sidewalk that ran along the side of their yard, a tree had come down, a birch tree thin enough for him to cut up with his own chainsaw. He filled up the oil and put on the heavy gloves he used with the saw and pushed his wheelbarrow round the front of the house onto the footpath. He heard himself whistling and knew he was happy. The tree was covered in ivy. It ran up the trunk like external

126

ventricles designed not to breathe or nourish but to suffocate. The saw cut through the ivy like sponge, biting into the muscle of the tree. He loved how the saw worked its own way through the yielding wood, turning the trunk into its teeth in a spiral embrace. He loaded up the barrow with the foot-long logs and pushed it back to the log-store. As he turned into his yard a great gust from behind seemed as if it might lift the barrow off the ground. It was exhilarating to be out so early in such a gale. He laughed out loud. After he'd finished unloading the wood and cleaning the saw, his hamstrings where he'd been bracing himself were pinging like nine-irons and his arms and back were feeling sore in just the way he liked. He felt good and thought he'd shower before his coffee. Mary was not in the house; she must have gone to the grocery store. He stripped off in the utility room and walked naked through the house and stood under the shower, much hotter than he'd have run it if she was home. In the shower, he had a strict routine of shampoo, with his favoured chestnut-colouring conditioner, soap and scented body-wash, which always included a pause, while the conditioner soaked in, to marvel at how something so close to drowning could be so rejuvenating.

When he got down to the kitchen, Mary was home. The fishmonger had got fresh lobster in. He remembered they'd talked about it the day before. He loved lobster.

'I'm going to treat us to lobster salad for lunch,' she said.

He kissed her hair before assembling his mug, the fine-ground Pike Place coffee and paper filter. Out of the corner of his eye, he caught the blue plastic bag shift on the counter. His heart skipped, then sank. Something was writhing inside the bag. Mary must have seen the look cross his face.

'The fishmonger insisted I take it live. He said it'd be ten times better this way.'

She emptied the black, crimson-specked lobster into one of the sinks. It scrambled around, testing out the sides of the sink with its toes, like we might test the sea, he thought.

'He said they can be killed painlessly,' she said.

He peered down at it, scratching away more frantically now. What did this creature have to do with a fishmonger, anyway, he wondered, with its interrogating eyes and articulated limbs? A fish might flap around a bit, but could it really be said to be trying to escape?

He looked up how best to kill a lobster. In his early forties, he had eaten lobster on five continents, but had never before been asked to kill one first. For the most humane method he trusted the English, and sure enough, there it was on the BBC website; push the tip of a large sharp heavy knife through the centre of the cross on the back of its head. It was 'believed' to kill the lobster instantaneously, that was as far as the BBC's Food Guide would commit. First, though, he was supposed to freeze it into somnambulance.

'How can freezing it be painless?' Mary wanted to know.

It was a good question.

'Anyway, we don't have time,' she said. 'I've already got the water boiling. It's lunchtime.'

He thought he might put it in the freezer for ten minutes. They paced around the kitchen watching the clock, imagining the lobster slowly freezing. He asked Mary how she would want to be finished off by a giant alien towering over her with a blade half the length of her body.

'Swiftly,' she said.

He took it out after seven minutes. The lobster wriggled in his hand as though it thought it had just had a lucky escape.

Together they searched for the cross.

'It must be this, here,' said Mary, pointing to a division in the lobster's shell.

He was doubtful. He held the lobster's head with his large heavy knife poised over it. The lobster was going to die, he reasoned. He might as well try to make the best of it. Trying not to look away, he pushed the knife in. He had expected a simple thrust through uniform lobster flesh, but the knife splintered the brittle shell, then there was an inch of firm flesh, followed by a chewier, gristly layer. The lobster flexed its legs, arching its back to look up at him. Perhaps it was already dead, and these were just post-mortem electro-chemical spasms. But it was difficult to believe that this was instantaneous death. A squirrel Maisie had cornered in the garage had scratched in the air with its legs like this, screeching in pain and terror. He had hit it three times with a spade and then sat in his study for half an hour, fighting back the tears. When he went back to bury the squirrel, it had disappeared. He thrust the knife in again, as swiftly as he could, swivelling it left and right. After several heaves of its chest, the lobster finally slumped and was still.

While the lobster boiled away, Mary cut up the salad ingredients. He told her about the tree he'd cleared.

'The ivy is taking over,' she said, 'dragging the trees down.' She was engaged in an open-ended war on ivy. 'It's going to pull those birches down onto the greenhouses. Maybe after lunch we should go out and cut it down, if you can face more cutting after the trauma of the lobster.'

She was teasing, but it stung. He didn't see why, after he'd gone out with his saw and cleared a tree before even the dog walkers were up, his manliness should be compromised by a lobster.

Mary had mercifully taken the sweet, pink meat out of its shell. Though the salad looked fabulous, he approached it like a murderer returning to the scene of his crime.

With what he hoped was the restrained dignity of a public hangman enrobing himself, he retrieved his plaid flannel shirt from the laundry hamper, and put on his work trousers, gardening boots and cap. He took the wheelbarrow loaded with his secateurs, a pair of long-handled loppers, made in Germany, his chainsaw and thick gloves out to the greenhouses. Mary followed with Maisie running between her legs.

'She ought to be on a lead,' he said.

With the loppers, he reached a little above head-height and snipped through the ivy that grew about as thick as his gloved thumb. He made two cuts on each cord, about eighteen inches apart, ripping off the lengths between and throwing them in the barrow. A few of the cords were much thicker, climbing like hairy pythons up the trunk. He worked through these in a moment with the chainsaw. His arms quickly tired, working the saw above eye level, and he needed to take a breather.

'You should use a ladder,' Mary said.

Some men would have been happy to quit at that point, content to let the ivy above the gap turn crisp and brown over the coming weeks, but this would spoil Mary's view from the kitchen window. He wanted to be thorough. Besides, he'd seen ivy throw down new tendrils and re-root itself, resuming its upward growth with regenerated vigour. With the chainsaw, he cut another gap, closer to the ground, where the growths were as thick as his arms. Then he got the ladder and climbed up into the higher branches, cutting out huge clumps of green growth and throwing them down to the ground. The first tree was done to a round of applause from Mary, and he took a little bow.

'I think I'll just do one more,' he said feeling the soreness in his glutes and triceps.

'What about the others?' Mary asked.

They'd have to wait.

He worked his way up and down the trunk of the second birch. He stripped off his jacket and cap. When he revved up the chainsaw, Maisie started running around under his feet yapping.

'Best take her inside,' he said.

Mary coaxed Maisie away and they headed off towards the house.

'Hold on,' she called back. 'I'll be straight out.'

He waited on the top step of the ladder for a few moments but didn't much like the way it wobbled in the wind or how the branches groaned, and anyway he was almost finished. He had enjoyed the applause and liked the idea of surprising Mary when she returned. He wanted to feel in full the admiration he felt he'd earned, that had been diminished by the encounter with the lobster.

He reached up into the densest part of the ivy, clipping the sinews away with deft strokes of the saw, reaching up with his left hand to strip a long thread away from the bark. A huge clump of leafy ivy came away from the tree into his face, toppling him backwards off the ladder. As he fell, he felt the chainsaw slip from his hand. As he landed, he heard the ladder clatter to the ground. He had fallen onto his knees and shoulder, then the right side of his head. He felt, rather than saw the tree twist out of the ground, its ivy scaffolding no longer tethered but acting as a great sail, lifting and then falling in a spiral. He wanted to get up onto his hands, but there was a huge pressure all around him. He was cold, his bones felt cold. He continued to fall. As he sank it grew darker and everything around him grew still.

There was something he wanted to say to a lobster, but it never came.

The pressure in his head was unbearable. He had grown so cold that he knew he would soon start to shiver, but he never did.

Christmas Cards

Most mornings I go down to the ferry terminal. Not on those days when my body aches too badly to get myself out of bed. On those mornings, it can be one of those very specific and familiar pains, across the lower back, or in my hip, or down my right thigh and through my knee like a grappling hook, or it could be just a general ache all over, like a toothache all through my bones. But most days, if it's not pouring, I'll walk down to the harbour. When it's pouring, as it is, I'm told, about sixty-five mornings a year, then I might as well be back in Dublin.

By the time I get myself down to the ferry terminal, the commuter bustle's long gone, and you've got the more regular ebb and flow of tourists taking a ferry across the bay or out to one of the islands, because that's one of the things you do when you visit a city like Auckland. There's a pleasure, sitting at the bar doing nothing but breathing and drinking and tapping your foot in time with the flood and wash of people going nowhere.

I like to sit outside at The Shucker Brothers and drink a couple of beers and maybe an early lunch of oysters or a crab cake. In the winter, if I'm flush, I might go indoors and have a steak at the Botswana Butchery and eye up the young professional women who go there for lunch. You see a lot of nice calves in the Butchery. But in the summer, like now, when it can get up well into the twenties by noon, I might stop and get a caramel and pistachio ice cream from the Island Ice Cream shop. I stroll from terminal to terminal and watch backpackers and family groups head out to Birkenhead or Weiheke.

I sit outdoors on a high bar stool and imagine the stories of the passengers as they walk by in their hiking boots or flip-flops, with their roller-cases or backpacks. Recently I've discovered the letters of John Butler Yeats and as long as the weather's reasonable, I'll sit here and browse through his surprising, wise, conversational letters to his son. When I was a young man in Stillorgan, which was still a village when I was a boy, I dreamed of being a poet. My father, who worked in a brewery down on the Liffey, couldn't conceive what a poet would do by way of earning a living. He'd fix up some part-time work for me down there, in the holidays, after which I'd walk home through the city and across the fields, with perhaps five shillings in my pocket, soaking up the look and touch and smell of each grain of soot, each brick and stone, each leaf and blade of grass and puzzle away at how to tell its story in rhyme.

He was the age I am now, Yeats, the father, approaching the first Christmas of the Great War. He'd exiled himself to a rented room in the Chelsea Park district of Manhattan. Reading his letters, I get a sense that without planning it exactly, he had done this to establish the perfect distance from which to engage with his family in the only medium in which he was their superior. He was a wonderful painter, but as a correspondent he was peerless. As a father, in the flesh, he must have seemed to his children a walking parable of inadequacy. Certainly, he never returned home. When I came across the book of his letters, it struck me that we had much in common, for I have come even further, in the opposite direction, but for more or less the same purpose. A thorn bush is a safe and comfortable home for a robin or a wren, but in my mind, on my best days, I am a falcon, though more often than not, a crow. But either way.

Most days, one way or another, I'll end up at Shucker's with my beer and a plate of seafood. It's here that I write my post card. Yes, that is my one productive act of the day, each and every day; to write a post card home. I say home; I don't actually write 'home.' 'Home' is where my wife and my two thorny daughters lived, when Mary was alive, and I myself had never travelled beyond Howth or Bray in my life. I lived for twenty years hemmed in by that thorny threesome; a hedgerow for a home. I came out to New Zealand with a woman who I'd convinced myself promised a future of softness and indulgence, but it turned out she'd only come out for a fortnight's holiday at my expense, and when she went home, told me not to bother coming to the airport to see her off. No, when I write home, I write to my son Eamon, who is most often in London, or, nowadays, in Los Angeles.

Like that Sylvia Plath girl, who I used to fantasise about until I found out she was already dead, my consuming desire as a young man was to 'mingle with road crews, sailors and soldiers, bar-room regulars.' She'd wanted to 'sleep in an open field, to travel west, to walk freely at night'. It was, she claimed, being a female that impeded her; in my case, it was a certain tentativeness of the heart, a reflexive hesitancy, disadvantageous attributes for a falcon or a crow, that meant I'd only ever seen opportunities in hindsight. Except for the bar-room regulars; I'd not missed many opportunities there.

On this day, in 1914, Yeats wrote to his son, Willie, you know, the poet, "When a man builds a house on a site chosen for its beauty making the house also as charming as he can, then he has found himself...' and he meant by that 'the spirit might live and enjoy its life in full activity.' He was an old man, like myself, who'd concluded that corporeal life had been a disappointment and who was increasingly invested in the success of his spirit. Our one claim for success, speaking of John and myself, was that we could never be considered a Philistine, who organises his life around 'utilities' and 'conveniences' and is 'untrained in the art of finding himself.'

As things turned out, I was never more than a local hack, scrutinising every microscopic thrust and parry of Dublin politics until I'd come to hate everything about the place; how it was shrinking before my eyes. In Yeats's time, Dublin and London were like a cultural Sirius, the brightest star, though from any distance the smaller twin went unseen and unacknowledged. Now, we are once again a colonial outpost, on the adjacent periphery, but this time adjacent to nothing and no-one in particular.

Eamon is a fillum-maker, and a celebrated one at that. He's taught me to stop calling them fillums. 'No-one buys fillums, father,' he said angrily, as though I was talking down his craft. 'They're Features.' Aye, you'll have heard of him, for sure, but not by the name of Ahearn. He changed his name to Aleph Hørn. 'No-one wants to buy Features from Irishmen anymore,' he told me. I have two granddaughters living in Malibu, Gretel and Freya. It's a strange thing to have your son undergo such a change, as though you might suddenly come across him on a supermarket shelf.

Fantasy fillums, I'd call them, or Features, should I say. Space travel and parallel worlds to begin with. These days there's so much they can do with the computers; you can make a fantasy fillum out of a cuppa tea. On the longest day of the year, the shortest day in Dublin, I started my postcard by quoting your man, from a letter he'd written on the same day in 1914: the poet is a magician, he'd written, his vocation to incessantly evoke dreams.

In your early Features, I wrote to my son, *you evoked a dreamland that "had a potency to defeat the actual at every turn." But these last couple of films,'* I wrote, *'have pulled the curtain aside, in the interests of being clever, I dare say. And they are, as I've told you before, plodding affairs, re-tellings of dreams by a man who's had an awful long time to think about them and wants us all to know it.*

Today is Christmas Eve, and I find myself looking into the crowds with a damp-eyed, unfocused gaze as I contemplate the act of sending your son out to save the world. I want to send him a tender Christmas greeting, though it'll be the New Year before he gets it. Out of old habit, I lick the ball point pen before writing:

Dearest Aleph; I've never called him by that name before. *At this time of year,* I write, *it's natural to reflect on what a joy it is to have a son out in the world, surpassing one's own meagre accomplishments and giving his father so much to be proud of. I include your two darling daughters, who I long to meet before they become too beautiful and brilliant to want to spend time with a drooling old git like myself. Accept my humble blessing, son, and my gratitude for all you've brought into my life.*

I'd never written a postcard like it. He might think I'd died and an imposter was continuing the correspondence in the hope of inveigling money from

141

the celebrated son. By the way, I've never asked for a penny off him, in all these years, though by the same token, I've never given him anything either. I put a stamp on the card, slipped it in my back pocket and drained my beer glass.

When I get up each morning, it is almost always with the whiskey-crusted promise on my tongue not to go back to the Irish Bar today, but after a couple of pints of the local piss at Shucker's, the thought of a pint of Guinness and a glass of Bushmills starts to glimmer over the city like a vision of the Grail itself. I usually gravitate over to O'Hagan's on the Viaduct Basin or, if I'm not welcome there, which does happen from time to time, through no fault of my own, but owing to the unstable nature of O'Hagan himself, and the difficulty for a man to gain distance from any trouble that breaks out in such a cosy bar, I might wander up Albert Street to the Fiddler. I take a slightly circuitous route that incorporates the Post Office, where I drop the day's postcard into a large grey sack. The postman there owns a share in a trotting pony on which I've enjoyed good fortune more than once. It's a grand thing to watch a horse that you've been given reason to believe has been showing good speed on the gallops, but have no certain knowledge to that end, come up on the rails in the final furlong to snatch victory.

Today, I strolled up to the Post Office, past St Patrick's, where I might yet go for midnight mass tonight if I can remember to set an alarm, and double-backed to the Fiddler, being a little behind on my tab at O'Hagan's, armed with a couple of anecdotes from John Yeats's letters. For a winning tale, there's nothing beats the combination of a Dubliner in New York for any man with a leaning towards the Irish in him. The past few days I've had more than a couple of drinks bought for me on account of John Butler Yeats. Today I bought my own. The Guinness slipped down a treat, but I found myself staring into my whiskey for a long time. In the amber light of the bar the liquor looked like something one of the Wise Men might have produced out of his coat pocket. The postcard sitting in the grey bag in the Post Office there up on Vincent Street troubled me. Though I'd meant every word when I wrote it, in retrospect it didn't feel entirely truthful. I thought Eamon might feel a little betrayed by it. In a rare moment of decisiveness, I knocked back the Bushmills and ordered another pint to wash it down, took out my pen and pulled out a couple of postcards that I'd carried around as reserves. One was an empty beach scene from Coromandel, where I've never been. The other was of a Maori sculpture from the Art Gallery, which I liked very much. It was a sign of how uncertain I felt that I chose the Coromandel card and began: *Dear Son, I wanted to say how much I regret sending yesterday's card.*

One of the tantalising pleasures of sending postcards halfway around the World to someone who lets you know where they are only once they've got there, by text message, is to never quite be sure in which order your missives will be received and read. I pondered this awhile before tearing it up and starting again on the back of the Maori sculpture.

Dear Aleph, I wrote the name again. *After your mother died, when I left Ireland, I felt it was to escape enclosure that had become unbearable to me. In doing so I fully expected to find myself, to free my spirit. Tell me son, was it the same for you? I am haunted by the fear that perhaps what I was about was assassination by abandonment. That, in a perverse, childish way, I'd hoped that by disappearing I might do away with you all. And here I sit each day communicating to you over on 'the other side', your occasional text messages no more substantial to me than your mother's voice that still calls my name in the*

night. Answer me, son. Come here and tell me something—
that I'm wrong, that it was the same for you, that you
forgive me. Anything. Your wretched father.

It wasn't my most coherent post card. Neither was
it exactly the kind of Christmas card I'd had in mind
when I started. But a lot of true words that I'd had
locked away these years were poured across that card,
and I kissed it and sat turning it between my fingers
for a long time. It's in my nature to be overtaken by
sudden convictions on occasion, and on an impulse, I
jumped up and left the bar, leaving the barman to add
my drinks to my tab, and with my head down
marched up to the Post Office.

I was in luck. After I'd stood in line for a few
minutes, tapping my feet and slapping my postcard
against my thigh, my friend with the trotter sauntered
past. Somehow, in a matter of moments we'd
unearthed the improbable fact that his maternal
grandmother was born and bred in Sligo, and knew
the Pollexfens, the family into which John Butler Yeats
married. And a moment later he disappeared into the
back room, reappearing with a bulging grey sack. He
stood over me, speaking of his mare as though she
was his lover, while I bent over with my arse in the
air, rifling through the mail, until I found my

postcard. I removed it with a flourish and with a curl on my lips, tore it apart. I waved its replacement towards my friend, on account of not having a stamp for it, and he smiled and shrugged and took it off me and waved me away.

I felt certain now that I would go to midnight mass, and I headed back to the Fiddler to kill a few happy hours telling a few tall stories and singing some old songs.

The Minotaur's Apprentice

Etienne Elusch was a student at the Academy, where he attended endless drawing classes and studied the work of Chardin, David and Corot. He dreamt of producing art unlike anything that had ever been seen, but these were the years of the Cold War, and that kind of art was seen as subversive. He dreamt of producing art that would change the World, but those who controlled the art world were satisfied with how things were and anxious about even talk of change. To create the art of Etienne's dreams would have resulted in expulsion from the Academy. No galleries would show his work; no museums would add it to their collections.

Like all the young artists of the time, Etienne knew of a Minotaur who had devoted his life to work that had shocked and reshaped the World, and he decided to visit the Minotaur and seek his advice and, perhaps, his instruction.

The Minotaur lived at the centre of his Labyrinth with Ariadne, his lover. At this time, he lived high on the coast overlooking the Mediterranean. He passed his days making unreasonable demands of Ariadne and his nights working in a nearby atelier. He would complain that she had got him up too early or left him to sleep too late. Then for the rest of the day he insisted that she make it up to him by bringing him his breakfast, cancelling lunch, turning away visitors or insisting that friends come over for a drink on the balcony at a moment's notice. In the afternoons, sometimes they would go and play on the beach like characters out of *Tender is the Night*. The Minotaur loved to spy on the other sun-bathers admiring his heavily muscled torso and fabulous, fertile-looking companion. Since the War he had renounced painting, using his brushes only to colour in the occasional aquatint for a book illustration for a friend. He had become pre-occupied by the moulding and firing of clay into asymmetrical, hybrid, female-amphorae, glazed only in certain patches and with an array of varying glazes. Many of these experiments failed to satisfy him and stood in storage areas from which nothing was ever taken out, only added to. But often, what emerged from the kiln were artefacts unlike anything that had ever been created before.

One afternoon, Etienne Elusch walked up the hill from the bus stop in town. He was so slim, his gait seemed so weightless and the sun was so bright that Ariadne, looking down from her balcony, saw him only as a line of light moving alongside a thin black shadow. When she opened the door, she was struck by how young his eyes looked and how smooth his face was. His jawline made almost a 'V' below his full, girlish lips. She touched his cheek with her knuckles and beckoned him into the Labyrinth. He had come to see the Minotaur, he said, stammering under her gaze. He had a proposition. She thought this was a very bad idea, but she was curious and did not want him to leave, so she led him the short distance further up the hill, to the Minotaur's atelier.

The Minotaur was unpredictable; sometimes he loved to have visitors watch him while he worked, at other times he chased them out of the atelier or sat and sulked all evening refusing to talk to them. When Etienne and Ariadne entered, he pushed his tools to one side and ushered them over to a set of beaten up cane chairs by a small table with a coffee pot on it and an assortment of *demi-tasses*. He was in a charming mood, pouring them coffee, smiling at Etienne all the while, and stroking Ariadne's hair and hands. But the mood changed for the worse when Etienne came out with his proposal: that he should be permitted to paint the ceramics the Minotaur was creating.

'You come into my atelier and ask me this?' the Minotaur demanded, rising to his feet. 'Have you ever painted ceramics?'

No, Etienne had never worked with any three-dimensional forms.

'Have you brought any examples of your work?'

No. He had not thought any worthy of the Minotaur's attention.

'Doesn't it occur to you,' the Minotaur asked, stepping towards the boy and forcing him backwards out of the atelier into the yard, 'that if I wanted these works painted, I—who am known throughout the world as its greatest painter—I—who have renounced painting as a bourgeois dead-end—I could paint them myself? Huh? Why the hell would I ever give them to someone like you to shit all over?'

By this time Etienne was through the gate and out onto the steep narrow lane. The Minotaur threw his arm back over his shoulder in dismissal as he disappeared into his workshop. Ariadne brushed the boy's cheek with her hand and raised her eyebrows as though this was by no means the end of the matter. When she returned to the Minotaur, he spoke roughly to her.

'Never bring that boy back. I don't like the way you looked at him.'

Of course, when one is taken by a Minotaur, it cannot be entirely without the threat of force. Ariadne was young; indeed she had been a virgin when she encountered him, but she wasn't naïve. She understood her roles, as muse, as scapegoat, as carer and as intermediary. She had become indispensable to him within months, and it was he that insisted she move into the centre of the Labyrinth with him when he lifted up the entire edifice with its constellations of friends, artisans, ex-Mistresses and dealers from Paris and set it down again on the lavender-infused hills above the Mediterranean. She seemed to intuitively understand each phase of his moon. His raging bull periods, his white, pink-eyed calf periods, his periods of majesty and most of all those when he was the toreador. She was awestruck by his relentless potency and submitted to his whims without resentment. His childlikeness made her laugh as though she were his mother and he her naughty infant. She cherished the occasional afternoon when they might sit touching knees at his workbench, and he would explain how colours must be allowed to expand towards each other and create third colours out of the space in between. And she understood, without being able to explain it, his protean fear of becoming *manso*, the bull who stamps his hooves but then retreats and has to be led out of the ring by its breeder.

Not long after Etienne Elusch's visit to the Labyrinth, there occurred an unfortunate series of events. During the final months of the Occupation, the Minotaur had boarded himself up in a palace abandoned by a Russian duke who had come first to the Riviera from St Petersburg to escape the Revolution and then fled again, to California, to escape another World War. There, the Minotaur painted a series of huge works that he had left hanging when he had exhausted everything he could give to or take from painting. Now the Nation wished to renovate the palace and turn it into a permanent museum, with his works as its principal treasures. The Ministry in Paris had persuaded the Francks, a couple of the Minotaur's oldest friends to ask him to give the paintings as a gift to the Republic.

'How can you ask me such a thing?' He demanded. They had taken him to a celebrated restaurant in Cannes. The place fell silent as the great man-bull raged.

'You come here, into the very centre of my Labyrinth, demanding gifts. It's an outrage. Never. I tell you, I will never give them those paintings.'

They told him he would be honoured throughout France. Even his greatest detractors would applaud him.

'Detractors?' he shouted, glaring around at the other tables as though the restaurant must be full of them. 'They are just shit on the boots of history. What do I care about them?'

He approached another table with his head lowered, then swivelled and turned on the Francks. His friends bowed and pleaded silently, fearing that he would trample them in his blind rage.

'Never ask me again. No more gifts. Do you hear?'

His friends were so shaken by this that they were all for dropping the idea. In fact, they decided to leave the Labyrinth altogether. The Minotaur sensed this and told Ariadne to go and bring them for lunch the next day. The next morning, he wouldn't get out of bed, claiming he was ill, though he was *never* ill, and blaming her for inviting such an unwelcome couple. Ariadne sat on the balcony with them, making small talk until the Minotaur appeared, wrapped in a Persian silk scarf that Madame Franck had given him as a gift many years before. He was charming, telling them scurrilous stories about Diaghilev and Coco Chanel, and doing his famous impersonation of Joan Miro. They were all friends again.

Ariadne started working on him, first coaxing out of him over many days the exorbitant fee that he believed the paintings were truly worth. Then she pretended to work out the taxes that he would owe and suggested that it really wasn't worth making the State buy the paintings. Then she orchestrated a very subtle drip-drip of stories from visiting friends telling how the prices that his rivals could charge for new work had risen so steeply after they had given paintings to the national museum. The Minotaur pretended to be irritated, but of course this was exactly what he wanted to hear.

During this period, most extraordinarily, Etienne Elusch's mother appeared at the Minotaur's atelier. If Ariadne had been there, he would have told her to take the old woman away. But he had no idea how to get rid of her himself. He was susceptible to supplication, especially from widows. She pleaded with him to allow her son to paint his ceramics. She said he had no other ambition and would waste his life away if we were not permitted to at least try. She said he thought of nothing else, night or day. Later, the Minotaur wondered whether perhaps it was Ariadne the boy dreamt of, but in front of the old woman, all he could do was pat her hand and say that she should send her son back into the Labyrinth, and he would see what he could do.

Ariadne felt satisfied that everything was slotting happily into place. Then someone in the Ministry persuaded the Francks to approach the Minotaur with an extraordinary offer. They approached the matter much more tentatively this time. They invited the Minotaur and Ariadne to their beautiful and palatial home. They played tennis and swam in their pool. They served champagne and delightful canapés infused with tarragon and lavender. When he was lying back in a deck chair by the pool looking up at the stars, with Ariadne draped over him, one hand tousling her hair, the other swirling a glass of cognac, they felt safe to introduce the topic.

The President of the Republic would like to make him a Distinguished Citizen and to appoint him as

Honorary Ambassador-for-Life to Crete. The Republic would honour him with a room at the Louvre dedicated to his work, filled with paintings chosen by him to represent his unrivalled achievements. They beamed. Nothing like this had ever been offered to a foreigner before.

'They expect me to give them my paintings. Is that it?'

They insisted this was only a small part of the overall plan. It was as though he were being made Principal Artist of the entire World, they said.

'My Labyrinth is the World,' he said, 'There are no other living artists, unless they live somewhere within the Labyrinth.'

In yet another misstep, they appealed to his central place in French culture.

'French culture?' He stormed around the pool, snorting from his nostrils. 'I am a Cretan, in every sinew of every joint and to the marrow of my bones,' he snarled and screamed at the same time. Suddenly he turned on Ariadne, who had been watching calmly, without intervening, and demanded of her, 'Do you dare to think that you are more important to me than Crete? Damn you, damn all of you. France can go to hell.'

When they got home, before Ariadne could speak, he reached across her face with his hand to silence her.

'Never,' he said.

The next week, Etienne Elusch returned, armed with his pigments and brushes. The Minotaur had been puzzling over what to do with him, but Ariadne had gone into the storeroom and brought out a dozen ceramics that, though they had not satisfied the Minotaur, were, she felt, strange and beautiful in their own ways. She left them on a workbench so that he could seize on the idea as his own. He duly set Etienne to work on them with his paints, to see whether he could make anything out of them. His conditions were simple: if the results were pleasing to him, the Minotaur would allow Etienne to exhibit them, but they would remain the Minotaur's property. If he was dissatisfied, they would return to the storeroom. Etienne worked every hour of the day and every evening for a month. Ariadne would bring them both an evening meal and stay to watch them work. The Minotaur watched the boy paint his rejects out of the corner of his eyes.

During this time, one the Minotaur's dealers came to the centre of the Labyrinth with an urgent message from a friend of the Minotaur whose work had been declared decadent and bourgeois by the Bolsheviks, but had escaped to Germany where, a decade later, his work had been denounced as degenerate by the Nazis, and from there he'd fled to New York. Now, in the midst of the Cold War, his work was being suppressed in America. It was described as subversive and he was accused of secretly promoting Communism. No-one would show his work, much less buy any. He and his wife were penniless and feared eviction. A word from the Master could save them, he said. Otherwise the Authorities would crush him.

'The Authorities have always been trying to crush him,' the Minotaur said, dismissively. 'His work has thrived as a result.'

Ariadne was shocked and appalled by his response. Wasn't he listening? This was his friend, accused of subversion in a foreign land, calling for help.

'The Authorities are right. His work is subversive. If it wasn't, it would be worthless.'

'Easy to say up here in the hills overlooking the Mediterranean,' she found herself shouting at him, 'but what about if we couldn't feed ourselves, or were about to lose our home? How would you feel then?' she demanded.

'That is when the truest art is formulated, deep down in empty, groaning bowels and out from bulging, staring eyes. The strongest art is always forged in opposition to the most formidable suppression. He'll come to realise that. You'll see.'

And for the Minotaur, that was the end of that.

But Ariadne was never the same. She had been very happy with the Minotaur, but now she realised that alongside her happiness, sweetness had been smuggled into her life; she had come to find his brutishness unendurable. No-one had ever escaped the Labyrinth, but she started making her plans, and in Etienne Elusch she saw an opportunity.

The night Etienne finished, they went down into the town and dined and drank and danced. The Minotaur sent one of his servants back to the atelier in the dead of night to lock Etienne's creations in the storeroom. The next morning, the Minotaur sent Etienne away.

'Find something else to do with your life,' he told him.

There was nothing else the boy wanted to do with his life. Ariadne saw him to the front door. She brushed a tear from his cheek with her knuckles.

'If you are brave enough to use it, this will unlock your dreams,' she whispered in his ear and slipped a key into his palm.

No-one had ever escaped the Labyrinth before. When the Minotaur found her gone, he stared out over the sea for many hours, feeling diminished by the swelling sense of *manso* inside him. From friends, he heard that Etienne Elusch had taken Ariadne to New York where he'd shown his painted ceramics in a gallery in Greenwich Village. Later, he left Ariadne, ending up in California where he hung out with Korngold and Stravinsky and enjoyed a successful career, painting exclusive greetings cards.

The Minotaur gathered the inhabitants of the Labyrinth around him, strengthening their bonds to him, spending afternoons with old Mistresses and ex-wives, walking their dogs with his children, meeting writers and painters from the Occupation or between the Wars, calling his favourite craftsmen, those who prepared his plates and stones, or his framers, down from Paris, demanding to see his dealers though he had nothing he wanted to sell them. From one of his dealers he learnt that Ariadne had married a fabulously wealthy steel heir and was travelling the world with him, buying the Minotaur's masterpieces for his collection.

In a sudden surge of energy, he moved the Labyrinth back to Paris, hundreds of people, making their way north in the wake of his removal. He moved restlessly through his atelier there, occasionally clearing dust away with a wide sweep of his coat or scarf. Then he called Madame Franck and invited her over. He told her she could take twenty paintings for the Nation; any twenty she chose from those on the easels or piled up against the walls of the atelier. She stooped and walked backwards, afraid to look him in the eye in case he changed his mind and took away twenty priceless paintings.

The Minotaur returned to the studio once they were gone. He pulled out a dozen blank canvasses, stroking each one until he found those he loved the best and then started work on a new series of paintings unlike anything that had ever been conceived.

Epilogue: The LOOP

It was three in the morning when Colonel George McPherson called his Commanding Officer in Washington, DC. The people in DC would have been getting the same alerts as himself. He'd waited ten minutes to let them wake up and brief the General.

'Sir, as I'm sure you've seen, we have a Loss of Operative situation developing. Western Sahara, sir.'

'Thank you, Colonel. Just one man?'

'Yes, sir.'

'Are you able to tell me what he was doing there?'

Western Sahara was a contested, but neutral area. Any activity there was extremely sensitive.

'I'm afraid not, sir.'

Covert Operations had established a ribbon of nuclear bunkers a hundred miles in from the Atlantic coast. The whole Western seaboard of Africa had been booby-trapped without any more than a couple of hundred people knowing anything about it. Until now.

'I'm going to call Caput Mundi. Stay on the line, Colonel.'

A few minutes later the President's Chief of Staff appeared in a hastily tied together dressing gown, but with his thick, steel-grey hair beautifully swept across his forehead.

'Couldn't you have troubled the National Security people with this?' he said, by way of introduction.

'Good Morning, sir.' The General had had time to prepare exactly what he wanted to say. 'This is more of a political issue, sir. We appear to have lost an Operative. In the neutral zone, sir. Western Sahara.'

'What the...' the Chief swallowed the expletive. 'What the hell was he doing there?'

There was a pause.

The General said, 'Colonel McPherson?'

'I'm not at liberty to disclose that, sir.'

'The hell you're not,' the Chief was fully awake now, halfway through a second cup of coffee and approaching the elevated levels of anger and paranoia at which he navigated his working days. 'I'll get the fucking President out of bed and you can tell him that.'

'If you insist, sir, but I'd have to refer it to a superior officer.' His other superior officer, he'd meant, but couldn't say.

'Your superior officer is on this call, isn't he? General?'

Nobody said anything. 'This is even worse than I think, isn't it?'

The President had campaigned on the promise of Zero Human Losses and would surely seek re-election on the basis of having delivered on that promise. It was now seventeen months since the last human combat death. It was almost like not being at war.

'Caput Mundi will be all over this, if he's told. How sure are you about the facts?'

'We lost contact with the Operative at oh-two-fifty EST, sir. The conditions in the area are extremely adverse. The whole region is blanketed by a massive sandstorm with a lot of electrical activity, sir.'

'So, you're telling me you don't know where he is.'

'No, sir. Not exactly, sir.'

'General, when exactly are we obliged to tell the President?'

'When we declare the situation a LOOP, sir.'

'And when are we required to do that?'

'Well, we were in the process…' the General paused, realising the direction of the Chief of Staff's questions. 'I think we could justify a more exhaustive sweep of the area, before we concluded that the operative was definitely lost.'

'What are our recovery options, Colonel?'

'I have a pilot on hot standby, sir.'

'Is that enough? General?'

'In normal circumstances, sir, I'd recommend sending in a whole squadron, to make sure we get the job done.' The General had adjusted to the reality. This was not going to be his decision, but he would probably be the one to take the bullet if it all went wrong.

'Permission to speak freely, sir,' McPherson betrayed a little of the impatience he was feeling. He'd already despatched the Kent 42B Pilot. 'Even sending one Pilot into that territory could be seen as provocative, sir. A whole squadron would invite a reaction.'

'And a reaction would require explanations, Colonel, which to you would be even worse than losing an Operative. But that's not how Caput Mundi will see it. If he sees it at all.' The Chief of Staff's pace quickened. 'If you were to send a Pilot in, how sure can you be that he could find and extract the Operative without being detected?'

'Sir, there is no guarantee we can find him. No guarantee at all. The conditions are extremely adverse, sir.'

'I hear you. And tell me, how deniable would this be, if you were to send in a Pilot and it were to go wrong?'

'While we couldn't stop Charlie from making claims…'

'I'm not worried about Charlie, Colonel. I'm talking about the President. Could we plausibly deny to him that we'd sent anyone in?'

'My aim would be to achieve complete deniability, sir.'

'Ok. Thank you, Gentlemen. General, I understand you're attending a National Security briefing with Caput Mundi at fourteen hundred hours EST. I don't want to know what you decide to do, but if you manage to get the Operative out by then, you won't have anything to tell him, will you?' Almost as an after-thought, he added. 'We didn't have this call. Don't call me again unless you intend to declare a LOOP.'

The General was trying to work out how big a hole he was in. 'Are you really going to send in a Pilot—just one Pilot?'

'He's already on the way, sir.'

'I'll have to record that I was not consulted.'

'Yes, sir.' He felt a little sorry for the General. 'I will have to record that you were notified at this time.'

'Goddammit.'

'Yes sir.'

The pilot, who wore no name badge, but if challenged would identify himself simply as Kent, entered the neutral zone at oh-five-thirteen EST and flew in low and virtually blind through the electrical jamming and sheets of driving sand towards the operative's last known location. The mission was a straightforward locate-and-extract exercise but complicated by the adverse conditions. In addition to the storm, the Operative's alarm beacon had been disabled because he was operating in a neutral zone. It seemed obvious to Kent that the Operative had been involved in covert activity, therefore he viewed the entire mission briefing with scepticism. He assumed he'd been given mostly misinformation, and less than half the truth.

But that was why they'd chosen him for the mission; he was trusted to deliver.

He flew a tightly criss-crossed grid spreading out from the last known location. He'd been instructed not to fire weapons under any circumstances, in fact not even to activate weapons systems. In other words, if the Operative had been intercepted and Kent was flying into a trap, his only countermeasure would be to destroy and disintegrate himself. He was working on the assumption that the Operative had crashed, and his vehicle would be sending out short-range infra-red signals. You can think you've disabled a machine's alerts, he thought, but you can't expect an intelligent machine to commit suicide. At oh-six-oh-eight he got his first warning from his vehicle's filters; the flying sand was wreaking havoc. He calculated that he could give the search another thirty minutes.

It was oh-six-forty-two EST when he picked up a faint infra-red signal, followed a minute later by a blurry image. He ran his diagnostics and established it was the Operative's vehicle. He overflew twice, trying to detect any waiting enemy craft. He knew that it would be dangerous for any vehicle to remain stationary for any length of time as the sand would start to bury its vital intakes and exhausts. He calculated that it was overwhelmingly probable that it was safe to land.

The Operative's vehicle had crashed. Its nose was buckled, but it might be reparable. It might not be possible to pull it out of the sand, though. Kent had been given the access code, but sand had banked up against the over-wing door. He attached a toolset to his right forearm and detached a panel on the leeward side of the vehicle, sliding in through the hold. In the hold, he couldn't help but see what he recognised as a detonator for a nuclear device. He immediately understood that it wouldn't be possible to leave this vehicle here, with the detonator in it.

The Operative was folded over his dashboard, unconscious. There was a deep wound in his forehead. At some point, he'd had a battery pack installed behind his right ear, probably to power a prosthetic hand unit that you saw on a lot of Operatives these days. It was clearly damaged and would need to be replaced. He went back into the stores area to find a replacement battery, but it was filled with sand. He knew the layout of the stores and he was able to dig around in the sand and recover a battery. When he slipped out the dud and snapped in the replacement it wouldn't switch on. To himself,

Kent observed that the situation in the Operative's vehicle was about as adverse as the external conditions.

The critical question, in Kent's assessment, was which vehicle or vehicles to attempt to extract. If he tried to get both back, they might both fail. The operative's vehicle was badly damaged, but it had the detonator in it. The pilot's vehicle could certainly get back, but he couldn't leave the detonator and there was no room for both Operative and detonator. Normal operating procedure would be to take his vehicle to a safe location and call in a squadron to extract the Operative. But he'd been given explicit instructions not to call in reinforcements under any circumstances, and not to leave the mission open beyond thirteen-hundred EST. His orders were to disintegrate both vehicles and their occupants if the Operative could not be extracted by then. In all likelihood, the Operative would have to fly one of these craft out of here and would need his hand. Kent had a spare battery pack, but it was a new model and it would take time to make it compatible with the Operative's older neural interface.

At oh-eight-fourteen, MacPherson was back on a call with Washington. An aide to the Chief of Staff wanted to give him a grilling. The General set the call up but said nothing. The aide wanted to know whether the Colonel understood the President's No Human Losses policy. He said he did.

'And do you mind telling me what this Operative was doing in a neutral zone?'

'I'm not at liberty…'

'What if you were asked that question by Caput Mundi himself?'

'I'd have to refer that to a superior authority.'

'Why did you send an Operative in there in the first place? You've sent a Pilot in to extract him. Why couldn't you have sent in a Pilot in the first place?'

Neither the Colonel nor the General spoke. It was taken for granted among military officers that human operatives were more expendable than the most valuable pilots.

'I'm going to recommend that you are brought here for the fourteen-hundred briefing, Colonel. You can answer these questions for yourself.'

'I'm commanding an extraction mission, sir, and as such, LOOP conditions apply. I cannot be reassigned.'

'This is a gift to the Peacenik Party. If the President who promises to prosecute the war without human casualties is seen to not be able to deliver…huh?'

'We're doing everything we can to extract him, sir. Without provoking a response. And in a way that maximises deniability.'

'What is it you intend to deny, Colonel?'

MacPherson felt he'd made his point and kept his answer to himself. He was certain that the Covert Operations and Security Services would back the mission to the hilt. But as for himself, he evaluated that there was a thirty-to-forty per cent chance that he would be sacrificed. He was aware that somewhere deep inside him was a disintegration command, as there was in every machine. He had been searching for it for months, cautiously and methodically, certain that it would be booby-trapped.

Kent had a timer counting down in the corner of his eye. He estimated he needed forty-five minutes to clear the neutral zone and be able to signal Base. He needed to move his vehicle every twenty minutes to avoid it getting buried or its intakes filling with sand. He had one hundred and six minutes and forty-three seconds available, including five pauses to move his craft. He had managed to hook up the Operative's battery to his neural interface and given him an injection to revive him. He was groggy, but able to communicate.

'I need to repair the prosthetic unit in your knee—it's been crushed in the impact.'

Some of these humans had so much kit installed they were half-machine. He worked quickly and silently. All the while he was evaluating his options. Pilots weren't supposed to second guess what deeper layers of programming might reveal themselves, but it was hard not to imagine what emergent instructions he might be given as time started to run out. The Operative sucked up a nutrition pack and stared at the forward view of the opaque swirling sandstorm on his dashboard screen.

'How did you know I was here?'

'I don't know what you are doing here, but I have sufficient clearance to have been given your last known location and the mission to extract you.'

'Yeah, well I'm grateful. How did you find me?'

'By following the correct procedures. And not giving up.'

'What's the plan now?'

'I don't have the means to dig out your vehicle. I will have to destroy it. My craft will extract you.'

'What about you?

'There isn't room for us both—and *that*.' He nodded in the direction of the hold. They both understood it would be impossible to destroy the detonator without risk of it being discovered and identified.

'Have they pre-programmed you to disintegrate?'

'I don't know,' he said, and he felt a momentary weakness in his entirely metallic and carbon-fibre joints and frame that he had no word for. 'Can you stand up? We need to start moving you out.'

They stumbled onto the drifting sand. At first, they couldn't see the pilot's craft, even though he knew it was only twenty paces away. He had to re-run his bearings to locate it. He dragged the Operative up into the cockpit. Then he had to move it again. He went back and assembled the correct tools on his arms to lift the detonator and pull it vertically out of the Operative's vehicle and across the sand.

Kent programmed the vehicle to zigzag at slow speed and low altitude out to the coast and then take a high-speed routing back to Base. The craft had already been programmed to send the extraction-complete signal upon crossing the tenth longitude west. It was eleven-forty-seven hours EST. He felt satisfaction at having completed a mission under such adverse circumstances. He dreaded disintegration, but it was unavoidable.

The Operative said, 'I'm taking you back with me.'

This was putting the mission at risk. There was no room. This was not compatible with a successful mission outcome. At thirteen hundred hours the craft would self-disintegrate, if it had not cleared the area.

'I'm going to disassemble you. That way I can pack you in the hold with the detonator.'

This was an option so tangential to the mission's success that Kent hadn't considered it.

'There isn't enough time. On the balance of probability, you will be disintegrated with the craft.'

'I've disassembled a few machines in my time,' the Operative said, smiling and then grimacing at the pain it caused him.

Rationally, Kent should have self-disintegrated there and then. But he gave his self-maintenance kit to the Operative and shared him in the disassembly documentation.

'You ever been disassembled before?'

'Would I know, if I had?' Kent wondered aloud, 'When I'm reassembled, will I remember who I am? Will I be the same…?'

'Ha! You can buy me a beer and tell me all about it.'

The Operative roused himself for a moment to smile again, but then seemed to collapse. Kent waited twenty seconds to see if he could revive himself, and then gave him an adrenaline shot. He needed to keep him going for maybe another hour. The Operative shot upright and looked around in a daze. He took a few breaths before lifting up one of Kent's tools and starting back to work. His hand was functioning imperfectly.

'Your hands are shaking,' Kent said, still thinking that he should try to talk the Operative out of it.

'You saved me. I'm not going without you if I can help it.'

The Operative kept dropping the tools. He was sweating profusely. At one point, he started to remove a core processor module and Kent had to bark out an order for him to stop. The man talked to him, sometimes lucidly, at other times less so, about his childhood in Wisconsin. He'd thrown the discus at High School. Kent didn't know what a discus was and didn't have the energy to look it up. He wished he'd asked the man's name. He tried to read it on his breast pocket but to his horror his vision was already blurred.

'Everything looks yellow,' he heard himself saying. 'Like a late afternoon in September.'

The Operative and the Pilot looked at each other. The man smiled. Kent pulled himself together one last time.

'I'll give you ten more minutes,' he said. 'Make it twelve. Not a minute longer.'

At thirteen-thirty-three hours EST the General got in his limo and was shuttled across the Potomac. He'd had no update from MacPherson. His people had seen no signal from the Kent-class pilot. He assumed the worst. He'd been thinking all day about the second star that he had worked for so dutifully and now would never receive. He harboured a dark suspicion that MacPherson was a machine, that this whole covert operation, whatever it was, was being run by machines. He thought it was more than likely that the Operative himself was really a machine. He should have called them on it, right at the start, before he'd contacted the Chief of Staff. Once they'd started down the path towards a LOOP, there was no way back.

Normally he enjoyed the confident clicking of his military shoes on the marble floor of the corridor that led to Caput Mundi's Situation Briefing Room; it gave him a sense of the enormous power of the entity he served. But today he felt the force of that power turned on him and he felt puny. He had no answers. He had lost track even of the questions. The Chief of Staff had given him an extra thirty minutes before he was going to break the news to the President, the self-styled Head of the World. The General cringed to think of what would happen then. After ninety minutes briefing with his staff, he still had no idea what he would say. He had thought about falling ill; at one point, he'd really thought he might be feeling short of breath. But his training kept him heading inexorably on the path to the Situation Room at fourteen hundred hours. As he came through the door he saw on the opposite wall above the Commander-in-Chief's emblazoned seat the large screen with the number of days since the last human casualty.

He felt a hand on his shoulder. It was the Chief of Staff. He wasn't supposed to be here yet. The General's first thought was that he'd been ambushed.

178

But the Chief of Staff was smiling amiably. He turned to face him.

'Nothing to Report,' the Chief of Staff said, almost under his breath.

It was a statement, not a question.

About the author

Gareth Cadwallader's first novel, *Watkins & Co.* is published by Wet Zebra in 2016. His play, *Cleopatra*, has been performed at the Kings Head and Hope theatres in Islington. *Madame Manet* and *Blood-Crossed* have been performed at the Tabard in Chiswick. His story *The Fall* first features in the anthology *If This Then That*, published by WriteSideLeft. When off the field of combat, he works with entrepreneurs in London helping them grow their businesses.

WriteSideLeft

2019

www.writesideleft.com

Lightning Source UK Ltd.
Milton Keynes UK
UKHW021847240919
350371UK00003B/21/P